Modern Critical Interpretations

Theodore Dreiser's
An American Tragedy

Modern Critical Interpretations

These and other titles in preparation

Modern Critical Interpretations

Theodore Dreiser's
An American Tragedy

Edited and with an introduction by

Harold Bloom
Sterling Professor of the Humanities
Yale University

Chelsea House Publishers ◊ *1988*

NEW YORK ◊ NEW HAVEN ◊ PHILADELPHIA

© 1988 by Chelsea House Publishers, a division
of Chelsea House Educational Communications, Inc.
  345 Whitney Avenue, New Haven, CT 06511
  95 Madison Avenue, New York, NY 10016
  5068B West Chester Pike, Edgemont, PA 19028

Introduction © 1988 by Harold Bloom

Printed and bound in the United States of America

10 9 8 7 6 5 4 3 2 1

∞ The paper used in this publication meets the minimum requirements
of the American National Standard for Permanence of Paper for Printed
Library Materials, Z39.48-1984.

Library of Congress Cataloging-in-Publication Data
Theodore Dreiser's An American Tragedy / edited and with an in-
troduction by Harold Bloom.
    p. cm. — (Modern critical interpretations)
  Bibliography: p.
  Includes index.
  Summary: A collection of eight critical essays on Dreiser's novel,
arranged in chronological order of their original publication.
  ISBN 1-55546-036-4 (alk. paper) : $24.50
  1. Dreiser, Theodore, 1871–1945. American tragedy. [1. Dreiser,
Theodore, 1871–1945. American tragedy. 2. American literature—
History and criticism.] I. Bloom, Harold. II. Series.
PS3507.R55A85 1988   87-22189
813'.54—dc19

Contents

Editor's Note

This book gathers together a representative selection of the best critical interpretations of Theodore Dreiser's major novel, *An American Tragedy*. The critical essays are reprinted here in the chronological order of their original publication. I am grateful to Hillary Kelleher and Paul Barickman for their aid in editing this volume.

My introduction denies the genre of tragedy to Dreiser's masterwork, and suggests instead that the relevant mode is pathos, which has its own, more severely limited possibility of aesthetic dignity. The chronological sequence of criticism begins with Ellen Moers, who searches out the prototypes in Dreiser's life for Asa Griffiths.

Robert Penn Warren, himself a major poet-novelist, renders homage to *An American Tragedy* as a dualistic "root-tragedy," finding Clyde tragic because he is a "mechanism with a consciousness." Considering the novel half a century after its publication, Robert H. Elias judges Clyde and Roberta to be exemplifications of the American loneliness endemic in the twenties. Donald Pizer, Dreiser's biographer, traces the origins of *An American Tragedy* in the Gillete murder case and in the *New York World's* reporting of the trial.

The effect of Poe upon Dreiser's novel is studied by Thomas P. Riggio, while Paul A. Orlov analyzes the book's narrative pattern, in order to explain how so inadequately crafted a novel nevertheless achieves such power.

Shelley Fisher Fishkin guides us "from fact to fiction," examining Dreiser's transformations of the Gillete murder case, creative changes that reflect Dreiser's principle that "fact is fate." In this volume's final essay, Philip Fisher deftly shows that Clyde is an imitation of a self, rather than a true individuality. Afflicted by "defective membership" in any context or group, Clyde can only adopt the stances and desires of others.

Introduction

The phrase that haunts Dreiser criticism is Lionel Trilling's "reality in America," implying as it does that *An American Tragedy* (1925) represents a rather drab projection of a dead-level naturalistic vision. More than sixty years later, novelistic reality in America extends rather widely, from Norman Mailer's not un-Dreiserian *The Executioner's Song* all the way to Thomas Pynchon's phantasmagoria in *The Crying of Lot 49*. Reality in America in the Age of Reagan includes Iran-Contragate, Jim and Tammy Bakker, and Modern Language Association conventions with scheduled seminars such as "Lesbian Approaches to Franz Kafka." Not even Pynchon can rival such inventions, and at this time Dreiser is in danger of seeming drabber than ever.

Irving Howe, writing in the midsixties, at a time of rising social protest, praised *An American Tragedy* for its grasp of the realities of American institutions:

> Dreiser published *An American Tragedy* in 1925. By then he was fifty-four years old, an established writer with his own fixed and hard-won ways, who had written three first-rate novels: *Sister Carrie, Jennie Gerhardt* and *The Financier*. These books are crowded with exact observation—observation worked closely into the grain of narrative—about the customs and class structure of American society in the phase of early finance capitalism. No other novelist has absorbed into his work as much knowledge as Dreiser had about American institutions: the mechanisms of business, the stifling rhythms of the factory, the inner hierarchy of a large hotel, the chicaneries of city politics, the status arrangements of rulers and ruled. For the most part Dreiser's characters are defined through their relationships to these institutions. They writhe and suffer to win a foothold in the slippery social world or to break out of the limits of established social norms. They exhaust themselves to gain success, they destroy themselves in acts of

1

impulsive deviancy. But whatever their individual lot, they all act out the drama of determinism — which, in Dreiser's handling, is not at all the sort of listless fatality that hostile critics would make it seem, but is rather a fierce struggle by human beings to discover the harsh limits of what is possible to them and thereby perhaps to enlarge those limits by an inch or two. That mostly they fail is Dreiser's tribute to reality.

That is rugged and sincere criticism, yet it repeats Dreiser's own tendency to identify reality with existent institutions, and to assume that reality is entirely social in its nature. "The harsh limits of what is possible" meant to Heraclitus (and Freud) a reminder that character is fate. Tragedy in America aesthetically can manifest the American difference, but that difference is hardly a naive social determinism. If *An American Tragedy* indeed is a tragedy, it requires something more than Howe asserts for Dreiser. Clyde Griffiths would have to have something in him that cannot be defined entirely through his relationships to social institutions. Howe, knowing that poor Clyde is rather puny, insists that Dreiser "nevertheless manages to make the consequences of Clyde's mediocrity, if not the mediocrity itself, seem tragic." Like Dreiser, Howe is a master of pathos, but the tragic cannot be a matter of pathos alone. It demands ethos (and Clyde has no character) and at least a touch of logos (and Clyde has no mind to speak of). I think we must defend *An American Tragedy* as a masterpiece of pathos alone, and I suggest we think of the book as *An American Suffering* or *An American Passion*. It then will require much less defense, and Dreiser's aesthetic permanence would not be questioned by critics who believe that the aesthetic is, after all, at least partly a matter of perception and of cognition.

Robert Penn Warren's homage to Dreiser shrewdly sought to defend *An American Tragedy* as a "root tragedy," naturalistic with the proverbial vengeance, "grounded in the essential human condition." Since Warren is a dualist who rejects transcendence, his view of Clyde is Cartesian: "A mechanism with a consciousness." It would seem that "root tragedy" is strong pathos, which returns us to the Passion of Clyde as Dreiser's true subject. That *An American Tragedy* has an authentic aesthetic dignity I do not doubt; rereading it is both a depressing and an engrossing experience. But I am persuaded that the critical defense of Dreiser, like that of Eugene O'Neill and indeed most serious American drama, depends upon restoring a sense of the aesthetics of suffering, which means of a sharing without transcendence or redemption.

In tragedy, the protagonist joins a beyond, which is a sharing with some sense of the Sublime. What Hart Crane nobly called "the visionary company of love" chooses its members, generally at very great cost. Clyde joins nothing, and would never have been capable of joining himself to anything, which is to repeat, in another range, Philip Fisher's insight as to Clyde's "defective membership" in any realm whatsoever. Pathos is universal, but it does not provide membership. That is the one certain principle of Dreiser's vision, maintaining itself into the moment before dying:

And then in the dark of this midwinter morning—the final moment—with the guards coming, first to slit his right trouser leg for the metal plate and then going to draw the curtains before the cells: "It is time, I fear. Courage, my son." It was the Reverend McMillan—now accompanied by the Reverend Gibson, who, seeing the prison guards approaching, was then addressing Clyde.

And Clyde now getting up from his cot, on which, beside the Reverend McMillan, he had been listening to the reading of John, 14, 15, 16: "Let not your heart be troubled. Ye believe in God—believe also in me." And then the final walk with the Reverend McMillan on his right hand and the Reverend Gibson on his left—the guards front and rear. But with, instead of the customary prayers, the Reverend McMillan announcing: "Humble yourselves under the mighty hand of God that He may exalt you in due time. Cast all your care upon Him for He careth for you. Be at peace. Wise and righteous are His ways, who hath called us into His eternal glory by Christ Jesus, after that we have suffered a little. I am the way, the truth and the life—no man cometh unto the Father but by me."

But various voices—as Clyde entered the first door to cross to the chair room, calling: "Good-by, Clyde." And Clyde, with enough earthly thought and strength to reply: "Good-by, all." But his voice sounding so strange and weak, even to himself, so far distant as though it emanated from another being walking alongside of him, and not from himself. And his feet were walking, but automatically, it seemed. And he was conscious of that familiar shuffle—shuffle—as they pushed him on and on toward that door. Now it was here; now it was being opened. There it was—at last—the chair he had so often seen in his dreams—that he so dreaded—to which he was now compelled to go. He was being pushed toward that—into that—on—on—through the door which was now open—to receive him—but which was as quickly closed again on all the earthly life he had ever known.

The enormous power of this is not necessarily literary or imaginative; Dreiser, like Poe, had the uncanny quality of being able to tap into our common nightmares. Compulsiveness dominates us here, but we cannot help seeing that Clyde cannot even join himself in these final moments. Like every crucial transition in Clyde's life, this is another mechanical operation of the spirit. The passion of Clyde embraces everything in us that is untouched by the will and the intellect. Dreiser is almost the unique instance in high literature of an author lived by forces he could not understand, forces that strongly did the writing for him.

Pure Religion and Undefiled

Ellen Moers

> *Pure religion and undefiled before God and the Father is this: To visit the fatherless and widows in their affliction, and to keep himself unspotted from the world.*
>
> JAMES 1:27

An American Tragedy, published when Dreiser was fifty-four, was the effective end as well as the climax of his career as a novelist, for in the remaining two decades of his life he would begin no new works of fiction and only with difficulty push himself to complete two long-standing projects for novels. Why Dreiser's last important statement as a novelist was a *Tragedy* is not known. None of his earlier books had resembled this work of the 1920s in its somberness, its pervading sense of evil, its theme of violent death. No earlier Dreiser character had aroused the fear and disgust that Clyde Griffiths does or possessed his power to destroy life. This marked change might be wholly attributed to Dreiser's advancing age and deepening radicalism, or to the spirit of the decade itself, except that the project for a murder novel and Dreiser's idea of The Rake were both more than twenty years old when he began to write the *Tragedy.* Whatever in its theme compelled and frightened Dreiser had been part of him for a long time.

What is Dreiser trying to say to us in this long and intense work? What is the meaning of the life and death of Clyde Griffiths, which he traces with such narrow, such relentless concentration through a hundred chapters and close to a thousand pages? Of all the ideas to which *An American Tragedy* can be reduced, none is simple, for Dreiser did not think simply. It was not merely that the ideas he drew from scientific authority, such as those of Loeb and Freud, were always being balanced and blended and opposed in his mind, but that no abstraction lived long in Dreiser's imagination without acquir-

From *Two Dreisers.* © 1969 by Ellen Moers. Viking, 1969.

ing personality. His most characteristic ideas were people-ideas, or idea-people; he was always referring to the impenetrable, unjudgeable qualities of real experience.

Is Dreiser trying to tell us that the social structure of modern America is vile, with its economic inequities and pervasive, though hypocritically denied, barriers between the classes? That Clyde's only true guilt is being poor and wanting to be rich, distinctions that are themselves morally wrong? That the capitalist system is more destructive of life than any individual murderer, because it places wealth and power in the hands of the worthless children of the Griffithses and the Finchleys (to whom a Clyde must attach himself as a parasite, in order to survive)?

Is Dreiser trying to tell us that all religion is a mockery, that there is no God? That Clyde's repressive religious upbringing is the guilty agent, for it fits him for no work, denies him self-fulfillment, forbids him the natural pleasures of the body, and fills his mind with false ideas? That the standard moral code pushes a helpless weakling such as Clyde toward a violent crime by denying him free sexual relations—and even (not a triviality) denying Roberta an abortion?

Is Dreiser trying to tell us that every man is essentially good, even a condemned murderer; that man's yearning for ease, luxury, and happiness is sound? Are we meant, throughout the harrowing finale of book 3, to pity Clyde for the agony of being tracked down, tried, jailed, and finally executed for a crime he did not commit? Is *this* the tragedy?

Or is Dreiser trying to tell us that the real tragedy of man is his powerlessness, of which he is not even aware? That the important human events happen in the subconscious, free of individual control, since the death wish and the sexual drives are fixed in the eternal character of the race? Or that those subconscious events are inevitable, tropistic reactions to physical and chemical stimuli? That man is little more than a machine, endowed (by some fluke in the structure of the neural colloids) with the illusion of movement toward a chosen goal?

Or did Dreiser write the story of Clyde Griffiths to show us what a killer is? Does Clyde represent the final human evil, just because he is stupid and weak? Is Dreiser trying to say that there is among human types one that, in its selfishness and greed, is indeed a blight, an adversary of life; that this type of man justifies the institution of capital punishment, which Dreiser refused to go on record as opposing; that the bad man exists, although he does not make himself evil—any more than does the poor Jew in *The Hand of the Potter,* whose homicidal lust for little girls is a chemical flaw in his genetic makeup?

Or is the story of Clyde Griffiths that of a willful fall from grace? Did Dreiser set his fable of the Unreal City in a Christian framework, beginning and ending with the family of street preachers, and opening and shutting the door of life on Clyde, in order to assert that for weak and strong, wise and foolish, Badman and Good, there is a true path as well as a Path That Leads the Other Way?

Or did Dreiser write *An American Tragedy* to say once again, more grimly than before, that there is no meaning, that the final horror is that of the unfathomable unknown?

Just before his execution, Clyde in the death cell ponders the impenetrable wall between his own inevitable craving for "things—just things" and his parents' blank condemnation of sins—just sins. "He had longed for so much there in Kansas City," Clyde thinks, "and had had so little."

> Things—just things—had seemed very important to him—and he had so resented being taken out on the streets as he had been, before all the other boys and girls, many of whom had all the things that he so craved. . . . That mission life that to his mother was so wonderful, yet, to him, so dreary! But was it wrong for him to feel so? Had it been? Would the Lord resent it now? And, maybe, she was right as to her thoughts about him. Unquestionably he would have been better off if he had followed her advice. But how strange it was, that . . . still he could not turn to her now and tell her, his own mother, just how it all happened. It was as though there was an insurmountable wall or impenetrable barrier between them. . . . She would never understand his craving for ease and luxury, for beauty, for love—his particular kind of love that went with show, pleasure, wealth, position. . . . She could not understand these things. She would look on all of it as sin—evil, selfishness . . . adultery—unchastity—murder.

In this fable of the Unreal City, no wall is higher, no door more firmly shut, than that between Clyde and his parents, between the seeking and the shunning of the evil in American life.

Clyde Griffiths's parents are the sort of people Dreiser always called "religionists": people whose testimony to the word of the Lord is overt, perpetual, and boring. They go about quoting the Bible and expressing unshakable confidence, quite without tangible justification, that the Lord will provide. Asa Griffiths, Clyde's father, is a gentle but half-crazed enthusiast who repeatedly exclaims, "Praise the Lord!" at the wrong moment—for example, when his daughter runs off with an actor. "Well, blessed be the name of the Lord. . . . Yes, yes! Praise the Lord—we must praise the Lord! Amen! Oh, yes! Tst! Tst! Tst!" Short, plump, and shabby, with bushy gray hair sticking out from under his odd round hat, Asa makes a strange appearance in the downtown streets of the city, where he leads the family in hymn singing and praying. Wholly ineffectual, he cannot lead them to schooling, training, or to anything like a suitable preparation for the worldly life.

Clyde's mother, Elvira Griffiths, a drab, shapeless, heavy-footed woman who wears some sort of makeshift religious uniform and bonnet, is almost as fervent an evangelist as Asa, and only slightly less impractical. Together they conduct a mission to the poor, where drunkards and derelicts exchange half-hearted testimonials to conversion for a little food and warmth. Ignorant but resolute in her faith, Elvira follows Asa into the city streets, where she plants her heavy feet and sings "resonantly, if slightly nasally, between the towering walls of the adjacent buildings,"

> The love of Jesus saves me whole,
> The love of God my steps control.

In 1920 Dreiser and Helen rented part of a house in a Highland Park neighborhood (then suburban, now downtown Los Angeles) that turned out to be full of bearded religious fanatics. One of these was their landlord, who lived upstairs. He had an odd way of interrupting casual conversations at inopportune moments by shouting "Praise the Lord!" Helen noted the fascination with which Dreiser studied the man, his angular, heavy-footed, nasal-voiced wife, who swayed awkwardly as she walked, and his teen-age daughter, who radiated physical self-consciousness. "Of all the households that we could have chosen," Helen later commented, "I thought this was one of the most singular, and yet, perhaps it supplied the necessary climate for the engendering of the soon-to-be-born *An American Tragedy.*"

"Engendering" is of course the wrong word for what Dreiser was doing to the materials of *An American Tragedy* in the 1920s, and wherever Asa Griffiths was born, it was not California. H. L. Mencken was sure, as usual, that he knew the source of the character: Dreiser's simple transcription from memory of a real religious enthusiast he had known in the early nineties. In the novel, according to Mencken, Asa Griffiths is "not first seen in Kansas City by chance: he is placed there because [*sic*] that is where Dreiser found him, far back in 1891 or 1892. I first heard of him" Mencken went on,

> in 1910 or thereabout, at which time he figured in a first sketch
> of the book that was to appear finally, more than thirty-five years
> later, as *The Bulwark.* Why he was transferred to *An American*

Tragedy I do not know . . . but I recall him clearly over all these years, for it was a peculiarity of Dreiser that his characters always lingered in memory, even when his stories faded.

Horace Liveright, Dreiser's long-suffering publisher, could have supplied Mencken with some details about the *Bulwark–American Tragedy* exchange in the early 1920s, but that too was not the engendering of Asa Griffiths.

Marguerite Tjader was sure she knew how old the character was, at least in his *Bulwark* manifestation, for as she worked with Dreiser on the novel in the last year of his life they came across a scrap of *Bulwark* manuscript on the back of a letter to Mencken, dated 1910. She was also sure of the source of the character, for Dreiser had specifically told her that "he had his own father in mind when he decided to portray a man dominated by religion and forced to face the modern world. This character must . . . be utterly crushed and defeated. . . . He has driven his children to opposite extremes, because of his own religious fanaticism." Of course, a minor change would have to be made: instead of a German Catholic the father would be a Quaker, because that, Dreiser said, was "more typically American."

Where Dreiser's interest in Quakers came from was no mystery to Anna P. Tatum, a Wellesley girl from Pennsylvania who in 1911 had written suddenly to Dreiser to say she was deeply moved by a story of his in *McClure's*—one of the *Twelve Men* portraits, about the Irish railroad foreman. The more Dreiser she read, the more he appeared to her to be the "American Tolstoy." "Do you know," she wrote him once, "I have believed in Tolstoy more since I have read you." Miss Tatum was the descendant of an old and distinguished American Quaker family, details of whose history she poured out to Dreiser, who was fascinated. In her own Bohemian existence she also demonstrated that Quaker traditions could push the modern young to rebellion. Anna Tatum did editing chores for Dreiser for years, especially on the Cowperwood books; she may even have discussed with him the fact that Charles Yerkes, the model for Dreiser's financier, came from a Quaker family (one detail that Dreiser did not use in *The Financier*). Years later, after her mother died, she gave Dreiser permission to go on with his novel about a Quaker banker, when his use of Tatum family material was no longer an embarrassment.

Edgar Lee Masters was sure he knew a good deal about the source of the character he called "the good man." On a visit to Chicago in 1912, Dreiser walked with his friend Masters up Michigan Avenue and went on for hours about the central character of what he thought would be his next book. "The good man who loved God," Masters wrote in his autobiography, "and kept his commandments, and for a time prospered and then went into disaster, had been selected by Dreiser for ironic portrayal." Masters contributed to the portrait many details about his own father-in-law, a man he believed to be much like Dreiser's "good man."

For those who remembered the Gillette case and knew how carefully Dreiser copied its record into the *Tragedy,* there was no question about why Dreiser chose an eccentrically religious family background for his murderers. Clyde's parents were evident copies of Gillette's parents. The senior Gillettes were religionists by profession; for a while they were involved with the Salvation Army and wore its uniform; they ran a mission in Denver; they lived for several years in a Christian Utopia called Zion City. When Dreiser settled finally on the Gillette case as his Rake matter, he began by writing a long introductory section (completed in California, and then cut from the *Tragedy* before publication) about the religious formation of Asa Griffiths and the Utopian community near Chicago which, in the one thoroughly happy period of his life, becomes Asa's home. Called the City of the Father on Dreiser's manuscript, it provides the Christian order, the communal fellowship, the sense of service and security that together make up Asa's ideal of contentment.

Readers of *Dawn* can have no doubts about the source of Clyde's religious home, for in his autobiography Dreiser wrote unequivocally that the "living prototype" of Asa Griffiths was a "defeated and worn-out religious fuzzy-wuzzy" named Asa Conklin. In 1890 Conklin had hired Dreiser (back from his year of college) to work in his inefficient Chicago real-estate office. A gentle, impractical old man, he cared nothing for business, everything for religion. Asa Conklin was "one of those ex-Civil War veterans or G.A.R. men, as we called them" who wore a baggy blue army suit with brass buttons and a wide-brimmed, low-crowned hat pulled down over his ears, from which his long, curly, white hair stuck out "most patriarchically and, may I add, foolishly." In the back of a mission on West Indiana Street (from its walls would be copied some of the mottoes for the Door of Hope mission in the *Tragedy*), Conklin lived with his wife, a woman as religious as he but somewhat more forceful, who actually ran the mission.

Dreiser spread out over seven *Dawn* chapters his recollections of this strange couple, whom he found both ridiculous and admirable. Their memory inspired him to a long diatribe not against all religion but against "those powerful and wholly practical and political organizations" such as the Catholic, Orthodox, and major Protestant churches, which in Dreiser's opinion have not only distorted Christianity by making it "a great, solid, material-seeming affair," in defiance of the spirit of the New Testament, but have also persecuted the smaller sects and the individual "lesser religionist" who try to worship and do good works in their own way. "Fortunately, there are others who . . . start up in religion for themselves, and . . . still serve God, do him a good turn, as it were, by gathering the forgotten straws and scattered grains in the master's vineyard, quite as did Ruth." Dreiser went on to state his own principle: the "best interpretation" he had heard of pure religion and undefiled was that given in the Epistle of James—" 'To visit the fatherless and widows in their affliction'—not when they are prosperous, mind you!— 'and to keep himself unspotted from the world.' "

This formulation of "pure religion" runs persistently through the whole span of Dreiser's work, for he relied on this simple biblical quotation more often, surely, than he himself was aware. We have already encountered "pure religion and undefiled" in the *Twelve Men* sketches written at the turn of the century: quoted by both the Doer of the Word and the Patriarch, it can stand as the central affirmation by all the Good Men of that collection. In the late 1920s, finishing *Dawn*, Dreiser cited "pure religion" as postscript to his account of the genesis of the Good Man figure in the *Tragedy*. And In the late 1940s he would place the same lines at the head of the final section of *The Bulwark*, where the Quaker father slips quietly into his final mood of resignation and acceptance. Solon Barnes, Asa Conklin, Charlie Potter; the fathers and forebears of Anna Tatum, of Chester Gillette, of Edgar Lee Masters, of Sallie White—and behind them, the captain of the *Sister Carrie* finale, another old G.A.R. man, another eccentric missionary to the poor—all stand surrogate in other places for the Asa Griffiths of *An American Tragedy*. All were both real and imagined, copied and invented; all are at once returns to and new departures from the kind of idea-person who fired Dreiser's imagination. The captain was a uniquely Dreiserian figure—and at the same time a real person, a phenomenon of the anxious nineties, when rich and poor drew apart from each other into a terrifying isolation unknown to the American twenties.

In the midnineties, as the Prophet of *Ev'ry Month,* Dreiser had called for a Redeemer of the modern city, who, "like the Nazarene of old," would need to "spring from the very humblest of the many, in order to appeal to and understand the many." He cried out against poverty's burden of misery and war, against the ruthlessness of success. He denounced the popular panacea of charity, for "there is no charity outside of that existing in the heart, the eye and the hand of one toward the suffering and woe of a visible *other*." In this blend of Populist rhetoric with Tolstoyan gospel, Dreiser spoke then— and would continue to speak—out of and for the American 1890s.

To the readers of *Ev'ry Month* in 1897, Dreiser had recommended that the ideal of the Samaritan be implanted in earliest childhood, and suggested that, in his own case, this had in fact been done.

> It is an ideal so commonplace that it is almost a necessity, and so perfect that, if struggled for, gives rise to almost every other virtue. . . . This is the ideal . . . of living the spirit of a social Samaritan, of, in short, working for the general good of others.
>
> At first it may seem as if this were not so much of a pleasing ideal, as one difficult and severe, but it seems so only to those who have never had it presented to them in their youth. . . . It is an ideal that is compatible with the teachings of every religion, and much more inspiring than the dogmas of most. It is one that appeals direct to the heart of the child.

Poverty and religion had been the dominant themes of Dreiser's childhood, as they are of Clyde Griffiths's. And in the Dreiser family, more than in most American (or European) families, the source of religion was the father. Because of John Paul Dreiser, they were all Catholics—and only because of him, for Mother Dreiser had been brought up a Protestant in the Anabaptist tradition at the other end of the Christian spectrum from Roman Catholicism. The Church was the obsessive center of Father's existence, reverenced with extremes of piety that, in family legend, were wryly attributed to a fall on the head that Father suffered in middle age. When he had money, John Paul seems to have given a disproportionate share of it to his Church; he even, Dreiser believed, gave the land on which St. Joseph's stood. When poor, the sick old man loved "to do the most menial work about a Catholic church . . . carrying in wood, building a fire. . . . You were nearer God and the angels," Dreiser wrote bitterly.

Father Dreiser had his ever-growing family of youngsters baptized and confirmed in the faith of his fathers, a somber, rigid, intolerant, and authoritarian German Catholicism. Most important, he insisted against opposition from both his wife and the children on their going to German Catholic parochial schools. Educationally as well as socially inferior to public school, these cost money which the family could ill afford. Dreiser long held on to the impression that church schools took a great deal of the family's money when there was any to take, but, when there wasn't, failed to supply the shoes for want of which the children could not go to school.

Of the German Catholic schools that Dreiser attended for irregular periods in Terre Haute, Sullivan, Vincennes, and Evansville, he kept none but disagreeable memories: of black-robed, hooded nuns who loomed "Gorgon"-

like over the classroom; of black-cassocked priests with German names, who "strutted or prowled" among the children; of Herr Professors who raised welts on their cheeks and palms with regular beatings; of church dignitaries to whom he had to raise his cap when he met them on the street, and say in German, "Praised be Jesus Christ." By his early parochial education Dreiser's style (if not his soul) was deeply marked, for the nuns taught him how to read and write German before English.

"My recollection of school and church life," Dreiser wrote in *A Hoosier Holiday*,

> is one confused jumble of masses, funerals, processions, lessons in catechism, the fierce beating of recalcitrant pupils, instructions preparatory to my first confession and communion, the meeting of huge dull sodalities or church societies with endless banners and emblems—(the men a poor type of workingmen)—and then marching off somewhere to funerals, picnics and the like out of school or church yard.

Dreiser took communion on Good Friday, 1945; but aside from that experience, and except as a tourist or for family funerals, he seems never to have entered a Catholic church after he reached manhood. Hardly a trace of his jumbled recollections of working-class Catholicism can be found in Dreiser's fiction—not the settings, the liturgy, the sacraments, the social atmosphere, not even, among his characters, the Catholics.

It was virtually impossible for the Dreiser children not to revolt. Their parochial education fitted them for nothing, Dreiser said, but a future as millhands and servant girls, destinies their father considered perfectly suitable for children of a poor man like himself. So Paul ran off from the seminary to the minstrel show, the girls ran off to Chicago, Rome hopped a railroad train. . . . To their father life was bounded not by the wide-open possibilities of booming America but by the narrow alternatives of heaven and hell, alternatives which "Catholicism had almost made a reality to me" by the age of eighteen, Dreiser wrote. (In 1939 he astonished a Quaker audience by saying that "up until I was forty years of age I believed fully that the world belonged to the Devil.")

Dreiser long remembered one of his father's dramatizations of eternal torment:

> I recall his once telling me that, if a small bird were to come only once every million or trillion years and rub its bill on a rock as big as the earth, the rock would be worn out before a man would

see the end of hell—eternal, fiery torture—once he was in it. And
then he would not see the end of it, but merely the beginning.

To such a hell, their father believed, all his American children were condemned.
In his heavy, sputtering, sometimes violent German-English style, he would
tell them every day of their childhood life that they would be damned for
neglecting the sacraments, and damned for a host of worldly sins which,
to the children, simply meant normal life on the American earth. Among
their sinful self-indulgences, according to their father, were dressing up,
drinking, loafing, theater-going, fiction-reading, dating, roller skating, and
spending money for the little nonnecessities that other children bought.

In milder moods, he must have nagged at them much as does the old
Jewish father, Berchansky, in *The Hand of the Potter* (the most sympathetic
and perhaps the most accurate of all Dreiser's father portraits). "Ice cream!
Ice cream soda! Who drinks dat? Poison, I tell you, poison—cornstarch.
Young people, dey must always be in de kendy-store, nowadays, spendin'
dere five-cent pieces." In his more violent moods, brought on by more serious
delinquencies, Father Dreiser must have sounded more like the German-
American butcher in Dreiser's early story "Old Rogaum and His Theresa,"
who locks his daughter out of the house for walking around too late with
her young man. But the full force of paternal wrath is evoked in *Jennie Gerhardt*,
where Father Gerhardt speaks in German to children who understand, but
answer in English. "By thunder!" he shouts, when told Jennie is pregnant,

"I thought so! . . . That comes of letting her go running around
at nights, buggy-riding, walking the streets. I thought so. God
in heaven! . . . Ruined! Ha! So he has ruined her, has he? . . . The
hound! May his soul burn in hell—the dog! Ah, God, I hope—I
hope—If I were not a Christian—" He clenched his hands, the
awfulness of his passion shaking him like a leaf.

Was this the man, with his rages and his pieties, who was the source
of Asa Griffiths or of "the personal act of forgiveness" that F. O. Matthiessen
found at the heart of *The Bulwark?* "The central truth" affirmed by Dreiser
through his creation of the Quaker father was, according to Matthiessen,
"that living authority lies not in the harsh judging mind but in the purified
and renewed affections of the heart."

"I can see him now," Dreiser wrote of his father, "in his worn-out clothes,
a derby or soft hat pulled low over his eyes, his shoes oiled (not shined) in
order to make them wear longer . . . trudging off at seven or eight every
morning, rain or shine"—and so far the recollection is evocative of Asa
Griffiths. But Dreiser goes on—"trudging off . . . to hear his beloved mass.

If some persons take to drink and others to drugs, a far greater number become addicted to religious formulae. . . . All of the impulses to live . . . are completely dissipated in appeals for mercy and spiritual salvation. Horrible! And to this are dedicated the endless religious edifices of the world!"

"I certainly had one of the most perfect mothers ever a man had," Dreiser wrote in *A Hoosier Holiday,* a work dedicated to his mother (as he thought of dedicating, but did not finally dedicate, *The Bulwark* to his father).

> A happy, hopeful, animal mother, with a desire to life. . . . A pagan mother taken over into the Catholic Church at marriage. . . . A great poet mother, because she loved fables and fairies . . . and once saw the Virgin Mary standing in our garden . . . and was wont to cry over tales of poverty almost as readily as over poverty itself. . . . A great hearted mother — loving, tender, charitable.

If the Samaritan ideal was implanted in Dreiser's heart from earliest childhood, it was the work of his mother, not his father, who, aside from his donations to the institutional church, was not a charitable man. But when there were beggars to be taken in, prostitutes to be befriended, sick people to be nursed, or tramps to be fed, "her large charity covered them all," as Dreiser wrote in an unfinished sketch of his mother called "Sarah Schanab"; for her tolerant acceptance of moral as well as worldly failure, of which her own children were the first beneficiaries, extended to the world beyond the family.

In all his autobiographical writings, Dreiser opposed his mother's gentle tolerance to his father's rigid piety, her love to his pride, her forgiveness to his harshness, her warmth to his dourness, her encouragement to his repression, her boundless charity to his mean thrift, her improvident generosity to his niggardly concern with paying off every cent on the dollar of old debts. Dreiser underlined these sharp, probably unfair contrasts by calling his father a religious fanatic, crank, and bigot and his mother a pagan. But "pagan" hardly describes the very special formation of Sarah Schänäb Dreiser.

She was born in a log cabin in Montgomery County, Ohio, in 1833. Not long before that her parents had migrated to the frontier from Pennsylvania. They were themselves Pennsylvania Dutch (more properly, Pennsylvania Germans), adherents of one of the German Anabaptist sects and thus "Plain People" like the Pennsylvania Quakers (to whom they were close in doctrine, if not in social position). Dreiser's maternal grandparents had personal and religious roots in Bethlehem, Germantown, and Beaver Falls; but whether they were Moravians, Mennonites, or Dunkards (sects where history is interwoven with those Pennsylvania cities) Dreiser never knew and his biographers have never ascertained. His mother's people may have converted from one of the sects to another and at some point become adherents of the United Brethren Church, a late schism (a Mennonite-Methodist compromise) in which two of Dreiser's Protestant uncles served as ministers. All Sarah's forebears, as far as she knew, were farmers, her parents prosperous ones, and she passed on to Dreiser her memories of rural abundance as well as of frontier simplicities. She could read but could not write until her children taught her.

To Sarah Schänäb's runaway marriage with a Catholic her parents were bitterly opposed, and they never spoke to her again. But she kept in close touch with her sisters and brothers, most of whom moved from Ohio to Indiana (in what Dreiser called "a kind of Mennonite migration of that day") and changed their name to Snepp. These Protestant aunts and uncles, including the two ministers, loomed fairly large in Dreiser's childhood, though he seems never to have met his Aunt Esther, a forceful, deeply religious woman who married a man of Quaker background and moved to Oregon. In the 1920s, however, Dreiser heard a good deal about Esther Schänäb from her granddaughter Helen, who would become his second wife. More speculative about the influence of family ancestry than he, Helen noted Dreiser's obsessive Bible-quoting, which became more pronounced as he grew older, and wondered "if he had not inherited some of the qualities of his mother's brothers who had been great Bible students."

Dreiser makes it clear that his mother did not discuss religious doctrine, a subject in which she bowed to the authority of her husband. A convert to Catholicism because of her marriage, she pressed the children to attend services, though she would have preferred public to parochial schools. And she died a Catholic in 1890, although there was then some difficulty with the Chicago priest, who tried to deny her a place in the Catholic cemetery because she had "neglected her duties of confession and communion for some time."

In one way, however, Sarah Dreiser bore witness to her lifelong tie with the traditions of the Plain People, and it was in a dramatic way—through her costume. All Dreiser's visual memories of his mother have her wearing the "plain dress" of the German Anabaptists—the long, patternless dark dress with turned-down white collar, and the tight-fitting prayer bonnet, which he sometimes described as "Mennonite," sometimes as "Moravian," sometimes as reminiscent of Quaker dress. He said that her costume fitted "her truly sacrificial spirit," and that it was "always suggestive of that Mennonite world from which she sprang, and so devoid of any suggestion of smartness, only simplicity and faith." These memories may have suggested the ugly brown coat and bonnet worn by Elvira Griffiths because of "some mood in regard to religious livery"—eccentricities of costume which to her son Clyde are "racking and disturbing things."

Prominent in all Dreiser's portraits of the "good man" is their affectation of a costume suggestive of simplicity and faith. They put on not the regulation uniform of an organization such as the Salvation Army or of a religious order but a makeshift affair—the oddments of Civil War uniform on Asa Conklin and the captain, the shabby round hat of Asa Griffiths, the sailor clothes of Charlie Potter. When Dreiser, in the late 1930s, first read the *Journal* of the American Quaker, John Woolman, he was once again impressed by a similar visual eccentricity, for Woolman had adopted for himself an idiosyncratic costume which outdid in simplicity that of the eighteenth-century Quakers among whom he went, crusading against slavery. Woolman, Dreiser wrote in *The Bulwark,* was a man "of poor and humble appearance, so eager to achieve simplicity and avoid worldly pretense and the belittling of any poorer human being by his own personal adornment that he wore garments of undyed homespun cloth, even a crude white felt hat."

Dreiser may well have known that the religious traditions of his mother's people, whether Moravian, Mennonite, or Dunkard, included an affirmation of early Christian principles at once more extreme and more ancient than that of the Quakers. Like the Quakers, the Anabaptists held their service (called Meeting) in a home or church building of strict simplicity. Like the Quakers, they elected their spiritual leaders from the community, calling them Brother. Like the Quakers, they rejected oaths, military service, personal display, and commercial trickeries. But unlike the Quakers, the Anabaptists were permanent outsiders to the American way of life. The German sects kept up, with varying degrees of rigor, the use of a low-German dialect among themselves, read a German Bible, and used High German in their services. Suspicious of trade for profit, the Anabaptists, unlike the Quakers, sanctified the rural life and manual labor long after such ideals had become anachronisms in American society. The similarity of the Anabaptist ideals to the Tolstoyan may have impressed Dreiser as it did Howells. In the first of his Tolstoy reviews, Howells had pointed out "that the Society of Friends, except in the single matter of heaping up riches, which they have been rather fond of, long lived the life [Tolstoy] commends; and that it is no new thing, either, in the practice of the Moravians, who were possibly somewhat nearer his ideal."

For American children of strict Anabaptist families, everything in daily life marked an opposition between the community of the faithful and the mysterious, dangerously tempting American world outside. There were rituals signifying belonging, there was discipline, which fell most harshly on the young, in matters of dress and amusement, and there were prohibitions against such material superfluities as the telephone, the automobile, and college. There was an education designed, like that of Clyde Griffiths, to teach the word of the Lord and almost nothing else. "Distinction between secular and religious education did not exist for these Brethren," writes the historian of Moravian communities in America. "None could be compelled to work for the Church, but all had to be either within or without its walls. . . . But most of the young Moravians knew no other world than the one . . . the fathers of the Church had carefully walled in. Their ideals of purity and piety in religion could best be realized by keeping themselves 'unspotted from the world.' "

Dreiser was not ever, least of all in *An American Tragedy,* the sort of novelist who set up sharp alternatives, arrived at clear choices, and wrote propaganda. "This propaganda idea has really been carried to an absurd conclusion," he wrote to a friend in 1938, by which time he had already made a political choice for the Communist left. "Only the other day some young writer was telling me that a man would write a better book if he had read and understood the Marxian dialectic! Imagine!"

He made no final choice between mother and father: his heart went out to one, his respect to the other, his obedience to neither. The life utterly dominated by faith was not something Dreiser bought and then in turn sold to his readers; it was something he accepted with wonder, for he had seen it lived by his father and by a series of eccentric "religionists" who crossed his path. He knew it brought peace, that it made trouble, that it spread charity, that in the American context it was ineffectual and thoroughly ridiculous. Dreiser, however, was not afraid of that ridicule which, as Jane Addams wrote of Tolstoy's example, "is the most difficult form of martyrdom."

Between his father's religion and what he knew of his mother's Dreiser did, of course, make a kind of choice, for the German Catholicism of school and church repelled him utterly and drove him forever from the formalities of institutionalized religion. But he did not at the end of his life become a convert to the Quaker faith, though his friendship in the 1930s with the distinguished Quaker leader Rufus Jones, his study of the Friends and their history, his immersion in the work of John Woolman, and his writing of *The Bulwark,* led many people to believe that he had done so. In matters of conviction, as in literary composition, Dreiser's development was circular and ruminative, not rectilinear and decisive. The resistant unworldliness of Anabaptism was bred in his bone, as were the authoritarianism and the hell-fires of his father's church. Dreiser would not have been the man or the novelist he was if his formation had not been in a real sense dialectical. This was as true in matters of faith as in those of social and scientific thought, of literary tradition, and even of nationality. "My father was a German," he once said, "my mother of Pennsylvania Dutch extraction. . . . I am radically American."

To the dilemmas raised with anguish and alarm in *An American Tragedy*, Dreiser offered no safe answers. He does not let us choose Good Man over Bad or believe that the faith of the one mitigates the threat of the other. Though the figure of the Good Man is present, one might say immanent, in all Dreiser's work, there Mr. Badman is his central concern—the seeking, erring, sinful, to him ever-compelling figure of American youth.

Dreiser did not choose between family interdependence and selfish youth; or between communal solidarity and the anarchy of American materialism. He gives us a world where no choice is free and the will is dead, but it is also a world through which run two paths, clearly marked: one that leads to salvation, and one that leads the other way. Dreiser's universe is godless and disordered, a gray fable-land of wasted lives and empty minds; it throbs with the passion of desire for trivialities, each as precious and as worthless as the jewels of Aladdin's cave.

Dreiser did not resolve the dilemma of "pure religion and undefiled," for dilemma it is, rather than an easy formula of a simple faith. The words Dreiser quoted so often present two distinct, for him unreconcilable challenges: one to the Samaritan ideal (to visit the fatherless and widows in their affliction) and one to unworldliness (to keep himself unspotted from the world). The first came easily to Dreiser, whether because he was a child of his mother, a product of the 1890s, or a disciple of Tolstoy it is not necessary to establish; and his greatest fiction (even more clearly than the Communism of his last years) is devoted to the gathering in of "forgotten straws."

But unworldliness was something else again. Dreiser was fascinated by the idea of the City of the Father, the absolute, walled-in refuge against the material life; he also deferred to the ancient wisdom he found in the narrow morality of repression and denial. But he could not reconcile either with his view of man as chemical mechanism, a view to which he adhered with religious awe. Dreiser accepted, he rejoiced in the Aladdin-like enchantments of American life, and he did not attempt to resolve the dilemma of "things" and "sins."

In Dreiser's fable of the Unreal City, no door shuts more firmly on the mysterious unknown than that which he calls the Door of Hope. This is the door toward which the boy Clyde and his parents make their way through the urban maze in the first chapter of *An American Tragedy*:

> The door of a yellow single-story wooden building, the large window and the two glass panes in the central door of which had been painted a gray-white. Across both windows and the smaller panels in the double door had been painted: "The Door of Hope. Bethel Independent Mission. . . . Everybody Welcome." Under this legend on each window were printed the words: "God is Love,"and below this again, in smaller type: "How Long Since You Wrote to Mother?"
>
> The small company entered the yellow unprepossessing door and disappeared.

Just as real, or just as fabulous, is the last door to open and shut on Clyde at the end of the novel. Again we see Clyde disappearing into it from behind, as if through the camera eye, as he makes his final progression:

> But various voices—as Clyde entered the first door to cross to the chair room, calling: "Good-by, Clyde." And Clyde, with enough earthly thought and strength to reply: "Good-by, all." But his voice sounding so strange and weak, even to himself, so far distant as though it emanated from another being walking alongside of him, and not from himself. And his feet were walking, but automatically, it seemed. And he was conscious of that familiar shuffle—shuffle—as they passed him on and on toward that door. Now it was here; now it was being opened. There it was—at last—the chair he had so often seen in his dreams—that he so dreaded—to which he was now compelled to go. He was being pushed toward that—into that—on—on—through the door which was now open—to receive him—but which was as quickly closed again on all the earthly life he had ever known.

Homage to *An American Tragedy*

Robert Penn Warren

An American Tragedy is the work in which Dreiser could look backward from the distance of middle age and evaluate his own experience of success and failure. We feel, in this book, the burden of the personal pathos, the echo of the personal struggle to purge the unworthy aspirations, to discover his own sincerity. We also feel, in this book, the burden of a historical moment, the moment of the Great Boom which climaxed the period from Grant to Coolidge, the half-century in which the new America of industry and finance capitalism was hardening into shape and its secret forces were emerging to dominate all life. In other words, *An American Tragedy* can be taken as a document, both personal and historical, and it is often admired, and defended, in these terms.

As a document, it is indeed powerful, but such documentary power is derivative: an artifact dug from the Sumerian tomb moves us not because it is beautiful but because some human hand, nameless and long since dust, had fashioned it; and a book may move us because we know what, of a man's life or of a moment in history, it represents. But the power of *An American Tragedy* is not derivative. The weight of Dreiser's experience and that of the historical moment are here, but they are here as materials; in the strange metabolism of creation, they are absorbed and transmuted into fictional idea, fictional analogy, fictional illusion. The book is "created," and therefore generates its own power, multiplying the power implicit in the materials.

The thing in *An American Tragedy* most obviously created is Clyde Griffiths himself. The fact that Dreiser, in his characteristic way, chose a model for Clyde does not make Clyde less of a creation. Rather, it emphasizes

From *Homage to Theodore Dreiser.* © 1971 by Robert Penn Warren. Random House, 1971.

that he is a creation; and the contrast between the dreary factuality of an old newspaper account and the anguishing inwardness of the personal story may well have served as a mirror for the contrast that always touched Dreiser's feelings and fired his imagination—the contrast between the grinding impersonality of the machine of the world and the pathos of the personal experience. In fact, the novel begins and ends with an image of this contrast: the family of street preachers, in the beginning with the boy Clyde and in the end with the illegitimate son of Clyde's sister Esta, stand lost between the "tall walls of the commercial heart of an American city" and lift up their hymn "against the vast skepticism and apathy of life." The image of the boy Clyde looking up at the "tall walls" of the world is the key image of the novel. And of Dreiser's life.

The creation of the character of Clyde is begun by a scrupulous accretion of detail, small indications, and trivial events. We are early caught in the dawning logic of these details. We early see the sidewise glances of yearning— the yearning he later feels when staring at the rich house of his uncle, and again when for the first time he lays eyes on Sondra, with "a curiously stinging sense of what it was to want and not to have." We see how, when he discovers his sister Esta in the secret room, his first reaction is selfish; how only when she refers to "poor Mamma" does his own sympathy stir; how this sympathy is converted suddenly into a sense of world-pathos, and then, in the end, turns back into self-pity. We see his real sadness at Roberta's jealousy, which he, also one of the deprived, can feel himself into, but we know that his pity for her is, at root, self-pity. We see him open the *Times-Union* to see the headline: *Accidental Double Tragedy at Pass Lake.* We see all this, and so much more, and remember his mother's letter to him after his flight from Kansas City: "for well I know how the devil tempts and pursues all of us mortals, and particularly just such a child as you." And what a stroke it is to fuse the reader's foreboding interest with the anxiety of the mother!

For Dreiser's method of presenting the character is far deeper and more subtle than that of mere accretion. The method is an enlargement and a clarifying, slow and merciless, of a dimly envisaged possibility. We gradually see the inward truth of the mother's clairvoyant phrase, "such a child as you"; and the story of Clyde is the documentation of this.

A thousand strands run backward and forward in this documentation, converting what is a process in time into a logic outside of time. When, back in Kansas City, we see Clyde's sexual fear and masochism in relation to the cold, cunning Hortense, we are laying the basis for our understanding of what will come later, the repetition with Sondra of the old relationship and the avenging of it on the defenseless Roberta. When, in the room of women where Clyde is foreman, he looks wistfully out the window on the summer river, we are being prepared for the moment when he first encounters Roberta at the pleasure lake, and for the grimmer moment to come on Big Bittern Lake. When, on the night after the first meeting with Sondra, Clyde does not go to Roberta, we know that this is a shadowy rehearsal for the last betrayal and murder.

It is not only that we find, in an analytic sense, the logic of character displayed; in such instances we find this logic transliterated into a thousand intermingling images, and in this transliteration the logic itself becoming the poetry of destiny. We see the process moving toward climax when, on the train, on the death ride with Roberta, Clyde flees from his own inner turmoil into the objective observations which, in their irrelevancy, are the mark of destiny: *Those nine black and white cows on that green hillside,* or *Those three automobiles out there running almost as fast as the train.* And we find the climax of the process in the "weird, contemptuous, mocking, lonely" call of the weir-weir bird which offers a commentary on the execution, as it had on the birth, of the murderous impulse.

This transliteration of logic into a poetry of destiny is what accounts for our peculiar involvement in the story of Clyde. What man, short of saint or sage, does not understand, in some secret way however different from Clyde's way, the story of Clyde and does not find it something deeper than a mere comment on the values of American culture? Furthermore, the mere fact that our suspense is not about the *what* but about the *how* and the *when* emphasizes our involvement. No, to be more specific, our *entrapment.* We are living out a destiny, painfully waiting for a doom. We live into Clyde's doom, and in the process live our own secret sense of doom which is the backdrop of our favorite dramas of the will.

The depth of our involvement — or entrapment — is indicated by the sudden sense of lassitude, even release, once the murder is committed; all is now fulfilled, and in that fact the drawstring is cut. With the act thus consummated, we may even detach ourselves, at least for the moment, from the youth now "making his way through a dark, uninhabited wood, a dry straw hat upon his head, a bag in his hand."

As a commentary of Dreiser's art, we can note how, after this sentence that closes book 2, Dreiser jerks back his camera from that lonely figure and begins book 3 by withdrawing into magisterial distance for a panoramic sweep of the lens: "Cataraqui County extending from the northernmost line of the village known as Three Mile Bay on the south to the Canadian border, on the north a distance of fifty miles. . . . Its greatest portion covered by uninhabited forests and. . . . " The whole effect is that of detachment; and with this we are restored, after a long painful while, to the role of observer, interested and critical, but not now involved.

But we shall not be long permitted to keep this comfortable role. Soon the camera will come close to the cell where Clyde waits, the focus will be sharpened. And in this constant alternation of focus, and shift from involvement to detachment, we find one of the deep art-principles of the work, one of the principles of its compelling rhythm. It is compelling because the shift of focus is never arbitrary; it grows out of the expressive needs of the narrative as Dreiser has conceived it, and out of the prior fact that the narrative is conceived as a drama involving both the individual and the universe.

Randolph Bourne once said that Dreiser had the "artist's vision without the sureness of the artist's technique." This is true of much of Dreiser's work, and in a limited sense may be true of *An American Tragedy*. I have used the phrase "Dreiser's art" in full awareness that most critics, even critics as dangerous to disagree with as Lionel Trilling, will find it absurd; and in full awareness that even those who admire Dreiser will, with few exceptions, concede a point on "art," or apologetically explain that Dreiser's ineptitudes somehow have the value of stylistic decorum and can be taken as a manifestation of his groping honesty, and will then push on to stake their case on his "power" and "compassion."

But ultimately how do we know the "power" or the "compassion" — know them differently, that is, from the power or compassion we may read into a news story — except by Dreiser's control? Except, in other words, by the rhythmic organization of his materials, the vibrance which is the life of fictional illusion, the tension among elements, and the mutual interpenetration in meaning of part and whole which gives us the sense of preternatural fulfillment? Except, in short, by art?

There is a tendency to freeze the question of Dreiser as an artist at the question of prose style. As for prose style, Dreiser is a split writer. There is the "literary" writer whose style is often abominable. But there is another writer, too, a writer who can create a scene with fidelity if not always with felicity. But often there is felicity, a felicity of dramatic baldness: the letters of Mrs. Griffiths or Roberta; the scene of Roberta back home, in her mother's house, looking out at the ruined fields; the scene when Clyde first sees Sondra, with that "curiously stinging sense of what it is to want and not to have"; the whole sequence leading up to the murder.

Words are what we have on the page of a novel, and words are not only a threshold, a set of signs, but indeed a fundamental aspect of meaning, absorbed into everything else. Words, however, are not the only language of fiction. There is the language of the unfolding scenes, what Dreiser, in the course of composing the novel, called the "procession and selection of events," the language of the imagery of enactment, with all its primitive massiveness — the movie in our heads, with all the entailed questions of psychological veracity and subtlety, of symbolic densities and rhythmic complexities. I am trying here to indicate something of the weight of this language, or better, these languages, as an aspect of Dreiser's art.

With this intention we can return to the question of the rhythm between detachment and involvement, which manifests itself in shifts of pace and scale. But we may find the basis for another rhythm in the fact that the personal story of Clyde is set in a whole series of shifting perspectives that generate their own rhythm. By perspective I do not mean a point of view in the ordinary technical sense. I mean what may be called an angle of interest. For instance, the picture of the organization of the collar factory in Lycurgus gives a perspective on life, and on the fate of Clyde; this is another contrast between mechanism and man, a symbolic rendering of the ground-idea of the novel that with each new perspective is reintroduced at rhythmic intervals.

But there are many perspectives. There is the perspective of the religious belief of the family, which returns in the end to frame the whole story; that of the world of the bellhop's bench in the hotel; that of sex and "chemism"; that of the stamping room in the factory with its mixture of sex, social differences, power, and money; that of the economic order of Lycurgus which stands as a mirror for the world outside; that of the jealousies and intrigues of the young social set of the town, jealousies and intrigues which, ironically enough, make it possible for Clyde to enter that charmed circle; that of justice and law in relation to the political structure of Cataraqui County; that of the death house.

Sometimes a perspective comes as an idea boldly stated, sometimes as implicit in a situation or person. In fact, all the persons of the novel, even the most incidental, are carriers of ideas and represent significant perspectives in which the story may be viewed. In the enormous cast there are no walk-ons; each actor has a role in the structure of the unfolding dialectic. And it is the pervasive sense of this participation, however unformulated, that gives the novel its density, the weight of destiny.

If, as a matter of fact, the dialectic were insisted upon merely as dialectic, we should not find this weight; and this is the great difference between the method of *An American Tragedy* and that of the Trilogy. In *An American Tragedy* the dialectic unfolds in personality, in the presentation of personality not as a carrier of an idea but as a thing of inner vibrance. The mother, for instance, is a small masterpiece of characterization. She is the carrier of "religion," but with her own inner contradictions, exists in her full and suffering reality, a reality which, at the end when she comes to join Clyde, affirms itself by her effect on everyone around. Roberta is fully rendered, not only in her place in the social and economic order and in her role as victim, but with the complexity of her humanity. When her friend Grace catches her in a lie about Clyde, she stiffens with "resentment," and this conversion of her self-anger into the relief of anger at her friend is a telling index, given in a flash, of the depth and anguish of her scarcely formulated inner struggle. She does not quite tell the truth to her mother about why she moves out of her first room. In the midst of her as yet submerged moral struggle, she deceives even herself as to why she selects a room downstairs and with an outside door in the new house. She is a sufferer, but she is not beyond the flash of jealous anger when Clyde, with unconscious brutality, remarks that Sondra dresses well: "If I had as much money as that, I could too." And the scene in which Clyde tries to persuade her to let him come to her room is of extraordinary depth, coming to climax when he turns sullenly away, and she, overwhelmed by the fear and pain at her own rebelliousness, feels the "first, flashing, blinding, bleeding stab of love."

Even minor characters have more than their relation to the dialectic. The prosecuting attorney and the defending lawyers have their own depths, and their roles are defined by their personal histories. A character like Hortense may be merely sketched in, but she takes on a new significance when we see her, like Rita, as an earlier image of Sondra, who is—and let us dwell on the adjectives—"as smart and vain and sweet a girl as Clyde had ever laid eyes on." And if at first Sondra herself seems scarcely more than another example of the particular type of femme fatale destined to work Clyde's ruin, let us remember how Clyde, in his cell, receives the letter beginning: "Clyde— This is so that you will not think someone once dear to you has utterly forgotten you." The letter, typewritten, is unsigned, but with it, in all the mixture of human feeling and falsity, Sondra, retroactively as it were, leaps to life.

As every person enters the story with a role in the dialectic, so every person enters with a human need which seeks fulfillment in the story. The delineation of this need—for instance, the portrait of the socially ambitious clerk in Lycurgus or the history of the prosecuting attorney Mason—serves to distract our interest from Clyde's personal story, to provide another kind of distancing of the main line of narrative. At the same time, in the extraordinary coherence of the novel, we finally see that such apparent digressions are really mirrors held up to Clyde's story, in fact to Clyde himself: in this world of mirrors complicity is the common doom. So here we have another version, in distraction of interest and realization of complicity, of the rhythm of approach and withdrawal.

There is, indeed, another sense in which the delineation of each new need compensates, in the end, for the distraction it has provoked. Each new need introduced into the novel serves as a booster to the thrust of narrative, each providing a new energy that, though at first a distraction, is absorbed into the central drive; and in the rhythm of these thrusts, we find another principle of the organization of the whole. Or to change our image, in the braiding together of these needs with the need of Clyde, we find a rhythm of pause and acceleration, the pulse of creative life.

To put the matter in another way, the delineation of each new perspective, each new person, each new need, serves as a new analysis of the dynamism of the story; for instance, the psychological makeup of the prosecutor, his frustrations and yearnings, are a part of the explanation of the course of justice. Each new element reveals a new depth of motive; there is a progressive "unmasking" of the secret springs of the action, related in the end to the "unmasking" of life as a mechanism cursed with consciousness, and something of our own resistance to unmasking enters into the whole response to the story. This resistance, set against our natural commitment to the narrative, creates another sort of tension, and another sort of rhythm of withdrawal and approach. Furthermore, over against the unmasking of the mechanism of life is set the feel of life itself being lived in the urgency of its illusions; and the play between the elements of this contrast gives us another principle of rhythm, another principle by which the form unfolds.

I have spoken of the marked moment of withdrawal at the beginning of book 3, after we have left Clyde walking away from the scene of Roberta's death, into the forest. Our commitment to the movement of narrative leading to the death of Roberta has been so complete that now, with the death accomplished, the story of the crime seems, for the moment at least, to split off from the subsequent story of consequences; and Dreiser, by the moment of withdrawal into distance, emphasizes the split. The split, coming about two-thirds of the way through the novel, has been felt, by some readers, to be a grave flaw in the structure. The split is indeed real—a real break in emotional continuity. But we must ask ourselves whether or not this split serves, as the similar "split" in Conrad's *Lord Jim* or Shakespeare's *Julius Caesar,* to emphasize a deeper thematic continuity.

The story is one of crime and consequences. In the first two books we see the forces that converge toward the death of Roberta, and in book 3 we see the forces that are triggered into action by her death; that is, we see the relation of the individual personality, and individual fate, to such forces as a continuing theme. But there is another and more general principle of continuity. The world in which the crime occurs is one of shadowy complicities, where all things seem to conspire in evil; the shadowiness of the outer world is matched by the shadowiness of the inner world. In such a world, what is the nature of responsibility? For instance, is Clyde really responsible for Roberta's death? At the very last moment in the boat he does not "will" to strike her—her death is an "accident." This "accident," to which we must return, ends book 2, but in the sequel the theme of responsibility and complicity are developed more fully and subtly, and the shadowiness of the inner world merges again and again with that of the outer. For instance, Jephson, one of the lawyers defending Clyde, creates a new version of the accident; and then Clyde is persuaded, without much resistance, to testify to a "lie" in order to establish, as Jephson puts it, the "truth."

This scene of the "persuasion" of Clyde is balanced by a later scene in which, after Clyde's conviction, the younger preacher McMillan strips Clyde of all his lies, alibis, and equivocations, and prepares him for repentance and salvation; in other words, McMillan asserts the idea of responsibility. But just before the execution, even as Clyde assures his mother that God has heard his prayers, he is asking himself: "Had he?" And Clyde goes to his death not knowing what he really thinks or feels, or what he has done. This theme of ambiguity—of complicity and responsibility—runs in varying manifestations through the novel; Clyde has always lived in the ambiguous mists of dream, and the most important thing shrouded from his sight is his own identity. In a world of shadowy complicities and uncertain responsibility, what is identity?

At the end, on death row, there is a little episode that asserts again the theme of identity in the novel. One of the condemned awaiting death is a man named Nicholson, a lawyer who has poisoned a client to gain control of his estate. Nicholson is clearly a man of breeding and education, and in spite of his criminality, has courage, humor, kindliness, and dignity. In short, he has a self that can somehow survive his own criminality and its consequences. His role in the story is a thematic one. He is set in contrast to Clyde—who has no "self"—and undertakes to instruct him in the rudimentary dignity of having an identity. When he is to be executed, he sends two books to Clyde, *Robinson Crusoe* and *The Arabian Nights*.

Here we find repeated the little device with which Dreiser indicates his meaning when he gives us the last glimpse of Carrie, sitting in her rocking chair with a copy of *Père Goriot* on her lap, the study of another "little soldier of fortune." As the novel of Balzac, whose fiction long ago had made Dreiser aware of his own role as the "ambitious beginner," so the gifts of Nicholson summarize the theme of *An American Tragedy*. The two books provide the poles of Clyde's story.

The significance of *Robinson Crusoe* is clear. It gives the image of a man who is totally self-reliant, who, alone and out of nothing, can create a life for himself, a world. Even in shipwreck — in disaster — he asserts and fulfills the self (as, we may say, Nicholson does).

As for *The Arabian Nights,* Dreiser does not have to trust the reader for a last-minute interpretation. At the trial, while Jephson is leading Clyde in his testimony, we find the following passage:

> "I see! I see!" went on Jephson, oratorically and loudly, having the jury and audience in mind. "A case of the Arabian Nights, of the enscorcelled and the enscorcellor [*sic*]."
>
> "I don't think I know what you mean," said Clyde.
>
> "A case of being bewitched, my poor boy — by beauty, love, wealth, by things that we sometimes think we want very, very much, and cannot ever have — that is what I mean, and that is what much of the love in the world amounts to."

In this passage Jephson summarizes the whole story of Clyde, but the summary has long since been prepared for in the novel. At the very beginning of his worldly career, in his "imaginary flights," the hotel where he was a bellhop seemed a magic world, "Aladdinish, really": "It meant that you did what you pleased." And this Aladdinish world, where dream is law, appears again at the very crucial moment of the novel when Clyde is being tempted by the genie, or Efrit, to the murder of Roberta:

> Indeed the center or mentating section of his brain at this time might well have been compared to a sealed and silent hall in which alone and undisturbed, and that in spite of himself, he now sat thinking on the mystic or evil and terrifying desires or advice of some darker or primordial and unregenerate nature of his own, and without the power to drive the same forth or himself to decamp, and yet also without the courage to act upon anything.
>
> For now the genii of his darkest and weakest side was speaking. And it said: "And would you escape from the demands of Roberta that but now and unto this hour have appeared unescapable to you? Behold! I bring you a way. It is the way of the lake — Pass Lake. This item that you have read — do you think it was placed in your hands for nothing?"

Notice that the genie's argument involves the notion that all is "done for" Clyde without his stir: the newspaper with the story of the death at Pass Lake has not been "placed" in his hands "for nothing." And this, of course, echoes Dreiser's analysis of his own need to have things "done for him"—which we shall come to shortly. Furthermore, we again notice here the situation of the self regarding the self, and the exculpation of self.

This is the world where dream is law and every wish is fulfilled effortlessly and innocently. The first Aladdinish dream, back in the Green-Davidson in Kansas City, had merely been to be like the guests of the hotel: "That you possessed all of these luxuries. That you went how, where, and when you pleased." Now the dream is different and dire; but the Efrit is ready still to show how it may be gratified, effortlessly and innocently, as in a dream. And the theme of the Aladdinish dream is merely a variant of the theme of identity—if wishes come true without responsibility, the moral meaning of the self is denied.

The fact that Dreiser divides the novel into only three books falsifies the intrinsic structure and blurs the fundamental theme. There are really four basic movements of the narrative, and there should be four books: the story up to the flight from Kansas City, that of the preparation; the story of the temptation leading to the death of Roberta; the story of the conviction, that of the ambiguities of justice; and the story of the search, as death draws near, for salvation and certainty as contrasted with ambiguity. In other words, the present book 3 should be divided; and then in the latter half, related to other themes, especially to that of Aladdin, but more deeply grounded, the theme of identity would be specific and dominant.

Throughout the whole novel this theme has been emerging. If in the world of complicities and ambiguities, it is hard to understand responsibility, then how, ultimately, can one understand the self? If one's dream is to "have things done for you," if one is passive, how can there be a self? In fact, in this world of shadows Clyde has always sought to flee from the self. In all his self-absorption and selfishness, he has sought to repudiate the deepest meaning of self. He had longed to enter the "tall walls" of the world and find there a dream-self, a self-to-be-created, a role to play in the rich and thrilling world—a *role*, we may say, to take the place of a *self*. The very end of book 1, which has described Clyde's first attempt to enter the world, shows him fleeing from the wreck of the borrowed car: "he hoped to hide—to lose himself and so escape." He wishes to escape responsibility and punishment; he does "lose himself," and early in book 2 we learn that he has lost his name, to reassume it only when he can use it to advantage with his rich uncle from Lycurgus.

All the rest of the story can be regarded as an attempt to repudiate the old self. And the repudiation of self is associated with Clyde's readiness to repudiate others: he is ashamed of his family; he drops new friends—Dillard and Rita, for example—as soon as he makes contact with his rich relations;

he ends by murdering Roberta. Or it may be put that Clyde, having no sense of the reality of self, has no sense of the reality of others; for instance, when Clyde assists Roberta into the boat that is to take her to her death, she seems "an almost nebulous figure . . . stepping down into an unsubstantial rowboat, upon a purely ideational lake." And as we have found earlier, even his pity for others is always a covert self-pity or a pity for the self that could not be, truly, a self.

At the end, in a last desperate hope, Clyde is forced by McMillan to recognize the truth that he has fled from responsibility and self. But even now, as Clyde tries to recognize this fact and thus discover and accept a self, he cannot be sure of who or what he is. His "tragedy" is that of namelessness, and this is one aspect of its being an American tragedy, the story of the individual without identity, whose responsible self has been absorbed by the great machine of modern industrial secularized society, and reduced to a cog, a cipher, an abstraction. Many people, including Sergei Eisenstein, who in his scenario, for a film that was never made, presents Clyde as the mere victim of society, have emphasized the social determinism in *An American Tragedy,* and James Farrell, in an essay on *Sister Carrie,* in *The League of Frightened Philistines,* succinctly summarizes this view:

> To him [Dreiser] evil is social: all his novels are concerned with social history, the social process of evil. Ambition, yearning, aspiration — these all revolve around this problem, and it in turn revolves around the role of money. He has related social causation . . . to the individual pattern of destiny.

It is one of the great achievements of Dreiser that he grasped and dramatized American urban society more strongly than any other writer. He did indeed relate social causation to the individual pattern of destiny, but deeper than this story of the individual set against the great machine of secularized society, is the story of the individual set against the great machine of the universe — the story we find in the image of Cowperwood, in prison, staring up at the stars, or in that of Clyde, after the death of Roberta, moving into the darkness of the woods. Furthermore, the contrast of man set against the universe is no more a complete description of his fate than that of man set against society. For man is not merely set against the machine of society or of the universe; he is himself a machine, and is set against the machine that is himself.

This was the doctrine that Dreiser, in the years leading up to *An American Tragedy,* adapted from Jacques Loeb, one of the pioneers in establishing the explanation of life by physiochemical laws subject to exploration by the methods of the laboratory. Under the tutelage of Loeb, Dreiser had come to feel that the stars that are indifferent to man, or would cross him, are not in the sky but in his bloodstream and nerve cells and genes; and that man himself is the dark wood in which he wanders. And this brings us back to Dreiser's theme of illusion.

Success, power, place, wealth, religion, art, love — over and over, in one way or another, in fiction or autobiography, Dreiser had defined each of these things as an "illusion." Now, in *An American Tragedy,* he specifically comes upon his final subject, the illusion of the self; for, whatever its origins, consciousness, with all the pathos of aspiration and desire, exists. The "mulch of chemistry" in man that gives him all his other illusions, gives him this, the primary illusion; and the drama of self-definition remains crucial. The last anguish is the yearning for identity, for the illusion that is the fundamental "truth," and Clyde Griffiths, now past all the other empty yearnings that had merely been masks for this deepest yearning, longs for this certainty as he walks down the corridor toward the fatal door at the end. But when, with his last "earthly thought and strength," he replies "good-by all" to the farewells of the condemned men whose turns have not yet come, his voice sounds "so strange and weak, even to himself, so far distant as though it emanated from another being walking alongside of him, and not from himself." What "self" he knows dissolves as now his feet walk "automatically" toward the door that would open to receive him and as quickly close upon "all the earthly life he had ever known" and upon the last illusion.

As soon as *An American Tragedy* was off the press, people began to ask what kind of tragedy, if any, it was. Clyde Griffiths scarcely seemed to be a tragic hero. He had not fallen from great place. He was not of great scale. Rather than being a man of action, he was acted upon. By what criteria might he be called tragic? Even readers who felt the power of the novel were troubled by the title.

The puzzlement was compounded by the notion that if Dreiser had used this title for his Trilogy (of which only two volumes had then appeared), nobody would have been surprised. Cowperwood, that is, appeared to be every inch the stuff of tragedy. If not of kingly blood, he was, like Tamburlaine, the stuff of which kings are made. His scale was beyond dispute, his power over men, women, and events preternatural. As for his ability to act, he was will incarnate in action. As far as the readers of 1925 were concerned, it seemed that one merely had to wait for the third volume to find the classic conclusion of a tragedy, complete with pity and terror; and even now, with *The Stoic* before us and the dwindling out of the hero with Bright's disease as the conclusion, we may remember that Marlowe's character, too, merely died a natural death, without losing his franchise as a tragic hero.

The comparison of Cowperwood and Clyde is essential for an understanding of what Dreiser is about in *An American Tragedy;* and it is reasonably clear that Dreiser himself was thinking and feeling in these terms. The hard, hypnotic, blazing blue gaze of Cowperwood, before which men quailed and women shivered delightedly, is the central fact of his image, insisted upon again and again. Clyde's eyes, too, are central for his image, and are insisted upon. In the very beginning, even as we are told that Clyde was "as vain and proud as he was poor," and was "one of those interesting individuals who looked upon himself as a thing apart" (as the young Dreiser had sung the refrain to himself, "No common man am I"), we see him studying his assets in a mirror: "a straight, well-cut nose, high white forehead, wavy, glossy black hair, eyes that were black and rather melancholy at times." It is those "deep and rather appealing eyes" that, when a girl cashier in a drugstore notices him, put him in the way of his first good job, in the Green-Davidson hotel. And when the other bellhops take him to his first brothel, the prostitute, trying to overcome his timidity, says, "I like your eyes. You're not like those other fellows. You're more refined, kinda."

Many others, including, of course, Sondra, are to feel the peculiar attraction of his eyes, but they are most obviously important in the stages of the affair with Roberta. There is the moment when she first becomes aware of the "darkness and melancholy and lure of his eyes" and, at the moment of the first kiss, of the "dark, hungry eyes held very close to hers." Then, in the magnificent scene when, after she has refused to let him come to her room and he leaves her standing in the dark street, she, in the "first, flashing, blinding, bleeding stab of love," thinks: "His beautiful face, his beautiful hands. His eyes." At last, on Big Bittern Lake, trying to steel himself to the deed: "And his dark, liquid, nervous eyes, looking anywhere but at her." And in the instant when she becomes aware of his strange expression and makes her fateful movement toward him in the boat: "And in the meantime his eyes — the pupils of the same growing momentarily larger and more lurid." And the last image we have of Clyde is through McMillan's memory when, after the execution, he wanders the night street: "Clyde's eyes! That look as he sank limply into that terrible chair, his eyes fixed nervously and, as he thought, appealingly and dazedly upon him and the group surrounding him."

The hard, blaze-blue glance of Cowperwood is the index of unrelenting, self-assertive male force. The dark melancholy gaze of Clyde is not an index of force: rather, of weakness, a device of blackmail by which, somehow, his weakness feeds on the kindly or guilty weakness of others so that pity is in the end converted into complicity. In *Dawn* Dreiser says that he himself had given way "to the whining notion that if something were done for me — much — I would amount to a great deal — a whimper which had taken its rise out of my self-exaggerated deprivations. . . . And which of us is not anxious, or at least willing, to have things done for him?" Cowperwood's glance is the mark of naked self-assertion, Clyde's gaze is a confession of the nonself—blank desire, a primal need to "have things done for him."

The self of Clyde does not exist except in terms of desire—at root the desire to create a self worthy of the fulfillment of desire, to conceal the sniveling worthless self. When Clyde sees girls "accompanied by some man in evening suit, dress shirt, high hat, bow tie, white kid gloves and patent leather shoes," he thinks: "To be able to wear such a suit with such ease and air!" And if he did attain such raiment, would he not be "well set upon the path that leads to all the blisses?" And so Dreiser develops, not by a woman but by a man, Clyde or himself, the philosophy of clothes that he had begun in *Sister Carrie:* now at a deeper level, an existential level, a level at which we understand the inwardness of the sad little tale of his embezzlement of $25.00 for the flashy overcoat and of his passion for fame, both as manifestations of the need to create a self, or to conceal the unworthy self.

To sum up, Cowperwood, with his brutal self-sufficiency, can make his way with women, but Clyde is like Dreiser, who could say of himself: "I was too cowardly to make my way with women readily; rather they made their way with me." So we see, for example, that Hortense, Rita, and Sondra "make their way" with Clyde; they have reasons for using him, Hortense for money, Sondra to spite the Griffiths of Lycurgus. Clyde, with his dark, melancholy eyes, merely happens to be handy. Roberta, too, in her own fashion, makes her way with him, as Dreiser quite explicitly puts it, for she has been seized by the "very virus of ambition and unrest that afflicted him."

Her own purposes, however shadowy and unadmitted to herself, are at work, but these purposes are transformed into love, while the purposes of Clyde, in his shadowy inner world of self-concern and self-deception, are not. Since Roberta is in love, and he is not, he can dominate her. But there is another factor involved here. Sondra is in love with Clyde too, and he does not dominate her; rather, with her he remains the passive yearner, the one who must "have things done for him," and it is appropriate that she talks baby talk to him. Underlying the difference between his dominance of Roberta and his subservience to Sondra is the difference in social scale. To Sondra, Clyde feels socially inferior, this feeling of inferiority fusing with his other feelings of weakness; but he has sensed that Roberta accepts him as a social superior who stoops to her, who can "do something" for her, and this feeling fuses with his satisfaction in his sexual dominance here achieved for the first time.

So we find, in the instant when Roberta, alarmed by the expression on her lover's face, moves toward him in the boat, this fundamentally significant sentence: "And Clyde, as instantly sensing the profoundness of his own failure, his own cowardice and inadequateness for such an occasion, as instantly yielding to a tide of submerged hate, not only for himself, but for Roberta—her power—or that of life to restrain him in this way." Roberta, the one woman whom he, as a male, has been able to dominate, now seeks to dominate him: she would thwart his desire. And in this instant of her return to the old role all women had had with him, he sensed the "profoundness" of his own failure—that is, his life-failure, his sexual failure—and the "submerged hate" bursts forth, and poor Roberta pays for all the pent-up and undecipherable hatred and self-hatred Clyde had found in those relationships.

The hate that bursts forth from its secret hiding place does not, it must be emphasized, eventuate in an act of will. Dreiser is explicit: "And yet fearing to act in any way . . ." If the hand holding the camera flies out, the gesture is one of revulsion and self-protection—of flight that somehow comes with an overtone of sexual flight. If Roberta falls into the water and drowns, he is "innocent." And here we are concerned with something different from a mere illustration of unconscious motive, for the episode has a deeper and more ironical implication in which the psychological dimension merges into the metaphysical. Clyde, the blackmailer with the dark, melancholy eyes, Clyde who wanted things done for him, Clyde the Aladdin with the magic lamp—now in this, the great crisis of his life, his deepest wish comes true. The Efrit has served him faithfully, to the end: "For despite your fear, your cowardice, this—this—has been done for you."

His wish is his doom. It is his doom in the deepest sense, for his "innocence" is here the index of his failure to have achieved a self, an identity.

To return to our question, if Clyde is merely the passive yearner who "wants things done for him," in what sense is his story a tragedy? The first stage toward an answer may be in the adjective "American," which is best explained by a remark, in *A Hoosier Holiday*, about the atmosphere of American cities that, Dreiser says, he has always missed abroad: the "crude, sweet illusion about the importance of things material"—the importance, as he puts it elsewhere in a passage already quoted, of "getting on." Clyde's dream is that "crude, sweet illusion," tragic in that for this mere illusion all values of life, and life itself, will be thrown away.

But behind this illusion is the illusion that in terms of "getting on" a self may be created, or an unworthy self concealed and redeemed. So here, again, as in the Trilogy, illusion is the key. With Cowperwood the tragic effect lies in the fact that the hero of great scale and force spends himself on illusion—the illusions of will, love, and art. But the hero who seems so self-sufficient, whose "blazing trail . . . did for the hour illuminate the terrors and wonders of individuality," is in the end only, as Dreiser puts it in the epilogue of *The Financier,* the "prince of a world of dreams whose reality was disillusion." So Dreiser, in Clyde Griffiths, turns his attention to another "prince of dreams." What does it matter if Clyde cannot achieve the "soul-dignity," the sense of identity, that Cowperwood could feel even when, in prison, he stared up at the indifferent constellations? What does it matter, for even that sense of "soul-dignity," though it is the illusion that is the only "truth," is but an illusion?

In the story of Clyde, Dreiser is trying to write the root tragedy. It is a tragedy concerned, as tragedy must be, with the nature of destiny, but, as the root tragedy, it seeks the lowest common denominator of tragic effect, an effect grounded in the essential human situation. It is a type of tragedy based on the notion that, on whatever scale, man's lot is always the same. He is the mechanism envisioned by Jacques Loeb, but he is a mechanism with consciousness. His tragedy lies in the doubleness of his nature. He is doomed, as mechanism, to enact a certain role. As a consciousness, he is doomed to seek self-definition in the "terrors and wonders of individuality," the last illusion and the source of final pain.

Some few human beings seem to avoid the doom, those who envisage a meaning beyond the natural order of life. For instance, Clyde's mother praying, on the night of his execution, for the soul of her son. In her prayer she affirms: "I know in whom I have believed."

Does she?

Theodore Dreiser and the Tragedy of the Twenties

Robert H. Elias

An American Tragedy is, by general agreement, Theodore Dreiser's major accomplishment. From Stuart Pratt Sherman and Joseph Wood Krutch to Robert Penn Warren and Ellen Moers, reviewers, critics, and scholars have praised its tragic impact, its moral effect, its technical artistry, its psychological depth. The book has been regarded as both the culmination of naturalistic possibility in the arts, concluding a nineteenth-century tradition, and the inaugurator of what is already another tradition, existential in its concern, addressing itself to our modern condition. Clyde Griffiths is the creature of fate, the captive of desire, the consequence of capitalism. He is the successor to Raskolnikov, the forerunner of Bigger Thomas, the anticipator of Meursault. The story is a story of the American mind, the Western heritage, the impossibility of absolute justice. Dramatists have transferred it to the stage here and abroad; Hollywood has twice given it a place in the cinematic sun, paying extraordinary prices for the privilege of mutilation first and adaptation second. Readers throughout the world have read it in either the original vulgate or in one of innumerable translations. It has been at once a critical and a popular success.

Biographers, too, have fastened upon this novel for what it discloses about Dreiser's own development. It was completed and published between the period in which he celebrated the individualistic struggle for survival and the period in which, abandoning his dedication to fiction, he committed himself to social reform that had as its object the limiting of individualism. It carries fragments of autobiography, sounds of Dreiser's voice, and formulations of Dreiser's preoccupations.

From *Prospects: Annual Journal of American Cultural Studies* 1 (1975). © 1975 by Burt Franklin & Co., Inc., and Jack Salzman.

In other words, *An American Tragedy* has interested critics for its timeless qualities or eternal themes, and biographers for its significant position in its author's career.

Yet there is another interest that must be recognized, one which in reference to *An American Tragedy* has usually been slighted: the interest of the cultural historian: It is but appropriate that on the fiftieth anniversary of the book's publication, by definition an occasion signifying our concern with the temporal, we should consider what Dreiser has told us about a moment of time, limited, identifiable, past: what, that is, he reflects as much as what he portrays. For although *An American Tragedy* surely has the timeless qualities that have been praised, and although Clyde Griffiths surely has the reverberating significance that relates him to earlier and later times, there are links to assumptions contemporary with the completion of the book that make the story and its protagonist very much a creation of the twenties.

The decade of the twenties was, as I have argued in "Entangling Alliances with None," a period in which the individual equated his freedom with an avoidance of entanglements with others. Whether one examines behavioristic treatises on child care, discussions of the companionate marriage, arguments in behalf of progressive education, relations between employers and employees, the presidents' views of their office, or foreign policy, one concludes that the twenties were years of atomistic individualism. The ideal was an individual who fulfilled himself hermetically: parents conditioned children not to quarrel, teachers learned to refrain from calling attention to adult standards, industry produced profits for absentee owners whose workers had no say in policy, chief executives minded their own business, and the nation eschewed international organizations that might gainsay its will. Individual and national sovereignty alike demanded the lone role. At a time when Calvin Coolidge and Charles A. Lindbergh, the Lone Eagle, were representative men, moreover, even the novelists at their most critical were unable to suggest ways of challenging public assumptions. Sinclair Lewis, John Dos Passos, F. Scott Fitzgerald, E. E. Cummings — not only did none of them create protagonists who could fulfill themselves by participating in their society; none of them could imagine a society in which fulfilling participation existed. Nor could the Harlem writers, who came closer to group consciousness than any others, seriously pose a self-limiting racial commitment as an acceptable alternative to the prevailing conception of unfettered self-reliance. One's own self-realization was, to state it briefly here, envisaged as incompatible with social involvement that affirmed the self-realization of others as a necessity.

It is this incompatibility that occupies a central position in *An American Tragedy* and this marks it as a book of its time. Published three years after

Babbitt and *The Enormous Room,* the same year as *The Great Gatsby, Arrowsmith,* and *Manhattan Transfer,* and only a few months before *The Sun Also Rises,* Dreiser's statement is essentially a tragic variation of the common theme, and Clyde Griffiths, although not like any of the characters in those other books, is still of their world.

The story of Clyde Griffiths is a story of a search for a society that will provide him with a place for the realization of his dreams but that regrettably must, as one of Dreiser's tentative titles suggests, remain a mirage. (Dreiser had once thought of calling the book *Mirage.*) Clyde is poor; his parents are strict; his indoctrination is otherworldly; but his wants are material and his desires secular and sensuous, if not sensual; and in a world where others have, and rise, and seem to live the good life, he yearns to become a part of the great show. His family is incongruous on the city's street corner. It is out of phase with history. It does not belong. Clyde needs to belong—to escape the isolation and loneliness that being different makes painful. He wants to be like others. If one can concur with the many critics who, taking their cues from F. O. Matthiessen and James T. Farrell, read Dreiser's novel as an ironic inversion of the familiar tale by Horatio Alger, Jr., one cannot at the same time refrain from asking what Algerian success means. I think that one finds that success for Alger is not just the acquisition of wealth, beauty, and power, but also the securing of a place in an ordered world within which human—personal—relations appear to be concomitants of individual fulfillment. If those relations sometimes are insubstantial or elusive, they nonetheless remain expectations in the realm of the possible. Dreiser's own characters in his earlier novels illustrate this.

Carrie Meeber, like many of her compatriots, moves from the provinces to the urban center. She regards herself at first as something of an outsider, but feels as she does only because she actually is from outside. She is not, as Clyde is, just "different." She is simply the innocent beginner among those who know better. Eventually she comes to know a little better, too. Although such knowledge does not insure either material power or spiritual satisfaction, she can still ask, still hope, still try to fashion out of images in the actual world a larger image that will answer to her dream born out of her capacity for wonder. Whether she will in fact manage to fashion such an image we do not know; we are urged to doubt it. But Dreiser himself does not confront Carrie or us with ultimate futility—only inconclusiveness— and we know that he even considered enlarging the role of Ames to give him an opportunity for a positive affirmation in the conclusion.

Likewise, Jennie Gerhardt remains excluded from only a small segment of society—society as defined by the successful. She is never the total alien.

Indeed, beyond any of Dreiser's other creations she is capable of genuine affection, warmth, self-sacrifice, and comes closer than the others to eliciting the response she deserves from those she loves. And that without any sense of shame or need for contrition. To give and to be are not for her incompatible.

Frank Cowperwood, too, for all his propensity to view people as simply coins of the realm, and women as, in addition, sex objects, is a man in society, where persons relate to each other more frequently than not. He does not give, but he is willing to assume risks, to acknowledge the reality of limits, to recognize that his will can be defined only insofar as it encounters the wills of others. He, like most of his nineteenth-century contemporaries, accepts his mortality.

But Clyde, despite his Algerian desire for money, clothes, and beautiful women, remains much further from the world of actuality. He moves amid abstractions — to fulfill his requirements he should be surrounded by well-regulated automatons — and in the view of others is ultimately an abstraction himself. Clearly Dreiser intends it to be this way. The world represented by Lycurgus is not a world in which people are affectionate and self-sacrificing; it is not a world in which the clash of wills is accepted as an exciting condition of life. Rather, it is a world that would banish difference in order to preserve the peace of rigidity. When one compares the attitude of Clyde's cousin Gilbert Griffiths, who wants to be safe in his position, with that of Gilbert's father, Samuel Griffiths, who retains a belief in struggle, one has no difficulty in seeing that Clyde's generation is living in a time that is a long way from the time of Charles T. Yerkes and even some distance from the time of the immediate prewar ferment.

Perhaps it is Clyde's relationship with Roberta that most forcefully dramatizes this aspect of Dreiser's theme. Clyde and Roberta are the only two lovers he shows us, and he takes pains to isolate both of them. Clyde is related to the rich but must work closer to the poor. He is permitted to hope that he can enter the circle of privilege, but he must "earn" his way. He cannot, however, earn it as though he were an ordinary worker attempting to climb the ladder of opportunity; for in the course of his efforts he must not disgrace the Griffiths name: he must act as though he were already arrived, not as though he were an ordinary laborer, like one of the foreign-born. In short, he carries the obligations of his lineage while he is excluded from the enjoyment of its emoluments. And Roberta, set apart from the other girls in the shop because she is "above" them in native endowments, fitted for something better but handicapped by an upbringing in an environment barren of opportunity and stimulus, is as lonely as Clyde.

Clyde is, in the chain of command, Roberta's superior, and in the light of what is required of Clyde that is a complication. Holding the position he does, he is not supposed to associated with someone in a position like hers. But eventually they come together and have each other — as a society of two, a tiny enclave in the larger Lycurgus. Yet more than any other enclave depicted in the other novels of the twenties, this one encounters menace. Jake Barnes, whatever one may think of the way he and his companions live in *The Sun Also Rises,* is part of a group that can after all maintain itself. Frederic Henry and Catherine Barkley can, in *A Farewell to Arms,* enact an idyll across the Swiss border, without regard for social sanctions, until only nature's dirty trick is played on them. Martin Arrowsmith finds hope with Terry Wickett on a secluded lake. Even Cummings's enormous room contains a group whose unity is not threatened with extinction by the state. Clyde and Roberta, however, live under continual threat. Their meetings must be clandestine. Their relationships must be at night. Their association is in its very nature incompatible with what Lycurgus values. They are, in fact, and especially when together, two of the loneliest characters in our fiction. In incident after incident Dreiser emphasizes that. Having brought them to intimacy to satisfy their emotional needs, he gradually forces them apart to satisfy Clyde's ambition to rise, and we observe how Clyde's understanding of rising, or social survival, leads him to overcome feelings, sever attachments, and shrug off loyalties. His growing separation from Roberta is marked by moments that Dreiser makes poignant. There is the evening at Starlight Park during which Roberta loses herself in gaiety while Clyde thinks of Sondra Finchley. There are the scenes in which Roberta fears that Clyde may forsake her while we readily penetrate his reassurances because we know that he is becoming emotionally disengaged. There is the dinner that they are to have together and that Roberta must eat alone. The two characters in the story who are seen in rare moments of incipiently genuine intimacy are finally destroyed by a world in which intimacy is irrelevant to survival. "Belonging" — obliterating the "differentness" that Clyde felt on the street corner of his childhood — comes to demand the repudiation of that community of concern that real belonging presupposes. Self-limitation and sacrifice have no status when self-realization requires the unconditioned will and fulfillment depends on disengagement.

Here society is an impossibility. If feelings are permitted, they can only intensify the pain of loneliness. I remember once, when Dreiser was introducing me to the symbolic drawings Hubert Davis had made for *An American Tragedy,* that he dwelt on the way Davis had shown how lonely Clyde and Roberta looked in their predicament and fear. And he was moved as he talked about it. Davis had obviously grasped the loneliness that lay at the heart of the drama.

I remember, too, arguing with a Soviet teacher of literature about the tragic aspect of the novel when she said that it really did not matter what happened after Roberta was drowned. Whether Clyde escaped or not, whether he was acquitted or not, whether he was executed or not, did not contribute to the meaning. Although I vigorously opposed her at the time, I now think that she was right in one respect anyway. Clyde has been said to have adopted the values of the larger society without ever learning how to make them work: success at all costs is good, but how to get away with it requires instruction; neither family nor state has ever told Clyde and Roberta about birth control, for example. Maybe so, but in another sense Clyde, when the boat tips, carries society's values to their logical conclusion and leaves nothing more to say. Overturning the boat in the way he does is the ultimate act of disengagement—the perfect severing of relations—and whether it was purpose or chance *must* remain in doubt; for that is what disengagement is all about. It is the work of careless people, or just indifferent people, people devoid of responsibility; it evinces the extinction of the involved will. Clyde's inner struggle, which contorts his face, is between a view of Roberta as a human being for whom a feeling still flickers and a view of her as an object that must be discarded for his freedom from fortune's hostages. And when what we regard as an accident plunges her into the lake, it is wholly fitting that Clyde lets her drown and thinks only about himself.

Dreiser, to be sure, makes the moment tremendously moving. Roberta's desperation, "that last frantic, white appealing look in her eyes," remains to haunt Clyde and us with an image of the very kind of feeling that has no chance in Clyde's world. That is the point. In such a world the commitment to the humanity of another is a subtraction from self. It is in dramatizing the inevitable futility of Roberta's appeal to Clyde's involvement that Dreiser objectifies his perception. For what arrests us is not that she is immensely pathetic but that Clyde in his adjustment to the conception of fulfillment that he has adopted is "conditioned" to withstand the pathos. This *is* Lycurgus; this is the America whose tragedy Dreiser's title announces.

There is a temptation to regard the book as a product of the time in which Dreiser first became interested in crimes like Clyde's. Dreiser himself said that his awareness of such cases dated from his stay in St. Louis when he was still a young reporter, and in his files are clippings and notes testifying that he collected material about these crimes fairly regularly before 1915. Moreover, as Ellen Moers has correctly noted in *Two Dreisers*, the taboos that prevail in Dreiser's Lycurgus are more characteristic of prewar America than of the decade in which the flapper hitched up her skirts, the young found Freud liberating, and Margaret Sanger disseminated knowledge about how to do it. One might even add that Clyde's career runs its course without many specific references to proclaim that he or anyone else lives among the consequences of the first World War. Nonetheless, we also know that even though Dreiser could adhere rather closely to the facts of the trial, he could not adhere to all the facts about Chester Gillette and Billy Brown, his principal prototypes. Despite his early fascination with the criminal act as a resolution to personal dilemmas, he did not manage to develop the implications of that resolution until time brought him the appropriate world. Hence, it was not until after the war that he was able to settle down to complete the story. The facts that he modified were those that would explain the nature of Clyde's aspirations and motives. Only when he could place Clyde in a context pervaded by the conceptions and values that flourished after the war could he make Clyde's catastrophe plausible to himself. The context had to lack convincing social alternatives. Indeed, Dreiser, reconstructing the past in the post-Wilsonian era, could not imagine, any more that Lewis or Hemingway could, the country's producing a society with such alternatives at the time; nor could he himself discover, any more than Cummings could, a personal recourse other than in art. (When a few years later Dreiser did suppose a new society might be brought into being, he forsook that art.)

Of course, *An American Tragedy* in much that it says fits nicely into the logic of Dreiser's life defined entirely apart from the historical moment. But one cannot avoid the impression that the particulars of the manifestation of that logic in *An American Tragedy* are inseparable from the historical moment.

It is then not too much to claim that Clyde's death in 1925 prefigured — and one should stress the "figure" here — the self-defeating consequences of the self-insulating society of the twenties: the retribution that was the Crash.

This was the tragedy of the twenties.

An American Tragedy

Donald Pizer

For more than a decade after the publication of *An American Tragedy* in late 1925, Dreiser often explained in letters, articles, and interviews that his purpose in writing the novel had not been to exploit the fictional possibilities of a particular sensational crime but rather to express an archetypal American dilemma. From youth, Dreiser recalled, he had been absorbed by magazine stories in which a working girl marries a wealthy young man or in which a poor young man marries well and thereby achieves prominence and luxury. In these versions of the American myth of success, marriage is a step upward socially and materially. Although youthful desire and effort might not gain immediate fulfillment, they would eventually be rewarded by a beneficent providence in one glorious act of recompense which combined love and success. By 1893, however, when Dreiser was a young reporter in St. Louis, he began to notice the prevalence of a crime which suggested the perniciousness of this myth, given the weaknesses of human nature. For in instance after instance, a young man resorted to murder when faced with the insoluble dilemma of a socially desirable match and an obstacle to that match. In the cases that Dreiser stressed—those of Carlyle Harris in 1893, Chester Gillette in 1906, and Clarence Richesen in 1911—this situation took a particularly evocative and "classic" shape. An ambitious young man just beginning his career forms a secret attachment with a poor, socially unacceptable girl. He then meets and wins a girl from a prominent and well-to-do family, but at that point his first love, "Miss Poor," announces her pregnancy and threatens to expose him to "Miss Rich." Attempts at abortion fail, and in desperation

From *The Novels of Theodore Dreiser: A Critical Study.* © 1976 by the University of Minnesota. University of Minnesota Press, 1976.

the young man murders his pregnant sweetheart and is eventually apprehended and executed. The "tragedy" of this kind of crime, Dreiser felt, was that Harris, Gillette, and Richesen were impelled primarily by the irresistible pressure within American life to gain success—to gain it honorably if possible "but any old way" if necessary. Gillette, Dreiser wrote, *"was really doing the kind of thing which Americans should and would have said was the wise and moral thing to do* [attempting to rise socially through the heart] *had he not committed a murder."* But because Gillette and the other two young men had not been resourceful or clever—because they did not know how to use contraceptives or how to get an abortion and because they did not have wealthy families to "handle the matter" for them—they had committed murder. They had thus been executed primarily for their inept attempts to fulfill the American dream by marrying "somebody with 'dough.'"

Although Dreiser in these later accounts of the sources of *An American Tragedy* always emphasized that the appeal of the Gillette case derived from its full and dramatic exemplification of a pervasive social reality, much of the attraction of the case, and others like it, lay in its evocative echoing of some of the most compelling realities of Dreiser's own life. For Dreiser, too, as a youth had felt oppressed by his narrow and poverty-sticken background and, instructed by the popular weeklies, had projected his daydreams of a better life and of sexual fulfillment into the hope of marrying well. As a lonely and lowly young man in Chicago, he comforted himself with the dream of marriage to a beautiful and wealthy girl. "I could see myself in gold chambers, giving myself over to what luxuries and delights." And a few years later, as an unemployed newspaperman, he gazed at the grandiose homes on Cleveland's Euclid Avenue, "envying the rich and wishing that I was famous or a member of a wealthy family, and that I might meet some one of the beautiful girls I imagined I saw there and have her fall in love with me." Although Dreiser did not find a girl with golden chambers or a house on Euclid Avenue, he did experience several rough equivalents of the kind of dilemma faced by Harris, Gillette, and Richesen. In the early 1890s he had won first Nellie, a fellow worker in a Chicago laundry, and then Alice, a salesgirl in a store. But after reaching the "lofty position" of a reporter, he met a "little blond" of far greater social position. "Because she was new to me," he recalled, "and comfortably stationed and better dressed than either Alice or N— had ever been, I esteemed her more highly, made invidious comparisons from a material point of view, and wished that I could marry some such well-placed girl without assuming all the stern obligations of matrimony." From 1893, when he met Sallie White, to their separation in 1910, Dreiser's personal life had the configuration of a permanent triangle.

Sallie was an unchanging base of drab and thwarting obligation, while in the green pastures of freedom were a seemingly unending chain of charming, clever, and wealthy women whom he was meeting through his work as reporter, magazine writer, an editor. No wonder that Dreiser indulged in the fantasy of killing off Angela-Sallie in *The "Genius"* and that his life with Helen Richardson, from their meeting in 1919 to their marriage in 1943, was marked by his constant efforts to limit severely the extent of his responsibility to her. In short, Dreiser's dramatization of the emotional reality of a wish to replace a "used up" woman with a more desirable one was as much a function of the memory as of the imagination.

Dreiser's novels before *An American Tragedy* can, in a limited but suggestive sense, be considered a search for an adequate form to represent his permanent preoccupation with the relationship between love and success. His interest in the myth of success took the form of studies of the variables in the basically unchanging pattern of "X" deserting "Miss/Mr. Poor" for "Mr./Miss Rich," a pattern in which wealth and position also implied a real or imagined "spiritual" superiority. So Carrie leaves Drouet for Hurstwood and then deserts Hurstwood with Ames in the back of her mind, while Lester leaves Jennie for Mrs. Gerald, Eugene seeks to leave Angela for Suzanne, and Cowperwood leaves Lillian for Aileen and Aileen for Berenice.

Dreiser also sought to express his interest in the myth of success in a number of studies in which the pursuit of Miss Rich leads to criminal acts. Of Dreiser's three such attempts before *An American Tragedy*, two survive in manuscript fragments and one is no longer extant. During the winter of 1914–15, Dreiser took extensive notes on the Roland Molineux case of 1899 and began writing a novel called "The Rake" based upon this well-known murder. A prologue and five chapters of this novel are in the Dreiser Collection. Then, toward the end of the decade, Dreiser wrote six now-lost chapters of a novel based on the Richesen case and almost completed a long story called "Her Boy" about a Philadelphia criminal.

Superficially, the Molineux case deviates from the pattern which most appealed to Dreiser, since it involved two men and a woman rather than a man and two women. Molineux had been courting a wealthy young girl. When a rival suitor appeared, Molineux's attempt to poison him resulted in the accidental death of an innocent woman. But Dreiser's depiction of Molineux as Ansley Bellinger is nevertheless closely related to his absorption in figures who commit criminal acts because of the irresistible pull of desire. Bellinger has an artistic temperament and is a lover of beauty, qualities which merge in his "keen passion for sex," but he is handicapped by a lack of money. He, too, therefore dreams of a romance with a beautiful well-born lady which will at once answer all his needs. When he encounters such a girl, he is sufficiently compelled by the demands of sex and ambition to attempt to kill the man who stands in his way.

"Her Boy" is about a young Irishman named Eddie Meagher who begins life with a weak and ineffectual mother and a brutish father. He drifts into petty crime and is at last shot while attempting to rob a bank. The source of the story was Dreiser's recollection of a Sullivan family and its bank-robber son. In recalling the background of the young man in *A Hoosier Holiday*, Dreiser remarked that he had "died a criminal in the chair owing to conditions over which he had no least control." In "Her Boy," Dreiser, who at this point in his career was much taken with the mechanistic theories of Jacques Loeb, added a further note to this deterministic theme by citing Eddie's "chemistry" as a vital factor in his life. Yet Eddie is no mere cipher.

> Intellectually he was destined never to be anything more than a clever artisan of some kind, though in the poorly combined substance of his chemistry, there were some registrations of beauty and possible phases of happiness which so early as thirteen and fourteen had begun to trouble his young soul—the beauty of girls, for one thing, the fine homes with their flowers and walks to be seen in other parts of the city—windows full of clothing, and musical instruments and interesting things, generally—things he had never known and was destined never to know in any satisfying and comforting way. For in spite of his poverty and all his need to bestir himself, Eddie's was still an errant mind, subject to dreams, vanities, illusions, which had nothing to do with practical affairs.

"The Rake" and "Her Boy" share an underlying theme whose presence in otherwise very different stories suggest its centrality in Dreiser's interest in the criminal as a fictional subject. Both Ansley Bellinger and Eddie respond to the beauty in life and both associate beauty not only with sex but with material possessions. Although one is intelligent, well-educated, and capable while the other is the opposite, both are dreamers who cannot brook the thwarting of their dreams. And out of this refusal there emerges a story of crime.

We do not know why Dreiser did not complete these various projects, but it is possible to speculate that each, in its way, failed to provide him with a satisfactory context for the representations of his basic theme. The Molineux case had a suitable protagonist but lacked the favored configuration of an old and new love. The action of "Her Boy" was too thin (Dreiser had only a sketchy awareness of the career of the Sullivan boy), and the background of the Richesen case no doubt centered too fully on the duties and world of a clergyman. (Richesen, a Massachusetts minister, had murdered his sweetheart in order to be free to marry a more suitable parishioner.) But in the Gillette case Dreiser had an almost ideal external shape for the expression of the themes which had preoccupied him in these tentative and abortive early efforts: a young man of limited background with an intense desire to advance himself; a triangle of a man and two women; and a fully reported crime of great dramatic potential.

Chester Gillette had murdered Grace Brown on July 11, 1906. His trial took place from November 13 to December 5, 1906, and he was executed on March 30, 1908. By late 1906, Dreiser had fully recovered from his breakdown of a few years earlier and was editing the *Broadway Magazine* in New York. He took considerable interest in the Gillette case as it was reported in the New York papers, though there is no conclusive evidence that he saved any clippings of these reports or that he planned at that time to use the case as the basis for a novel.

The period between Dreiser's completion of *The Titan* in late 1913 and his early work on *An American Tragedy* in mid-1920 was one of intense literary productivity but little sustained work on any single novel. It was a period of many new literary interests — in drama, poetry, autobiography, and philosophical essays; of discouragement about the possibility of making a living as a novelist after the financial failure of *The Titan* in 1915 and the suppression of *The "Genius"* in 1916; and of an inability to proceed with such planned long works as "The Rake" and *The Bulwark*. In September 1919, Dreiser met Helen Richardson and in October moved with her to Los Angeles, where Dreiser hoped to complete *The Bulwark* for spring publication by his new publisher, Boni and Liveright. During the winter and spring of 1919–20, Dreiser continued to work sporadically on *The Bulwark* as well as on the second volume of his autobiography and a new collection of short stories. We do not know precisely when he began work on *An American Tragedy*, but a rough date is the late summer of 1920. In a letter of August 13, 1920, to Mencken he outlined his literary activities in some detail but failed to ˙mention a new project. Yet on the same day he also wrote the district attorney of Herkimer County, New York, to inquire about the availability of the verbatim record of the Gillette trial. And on December 3, 1920, he wrote Liveright that he had begun work on a new novel "sometime ago" and that he hoped to finish it in April. In fact, however, this project also faltered (for reasons I shall discuss later), and when Dreiser left Los Angeles for New York in November 1922, he had completed only twenty chapters of *An American Tragedy*.

Dreiser's notes for *An American Tragedy* have not survived, but he depended heavily and explicitly in the final version of the novel on the extensive coverage of the trial and its aftermath in the *New York World*. A file of the *World*, however, was not available to him in Los Angeles. And since the trial record of the Gillette case comprised three bulky volumes, it is extremely unlikely that his request for a copy was honored. He therefore relied in California either on clippings of the case sent to him from New York or on the lengthy accounts of the trial in the Los Angeles papers of 1906. From these sources, Dreiser learned that Gillette had been raised haphazardly by his missionary parents as they moved from one Western town to another and that at the age of fourteen he had left his parents for a series of miscellaneous jobs. At eighteen he had attended Oberlin College for two years, supported both by his parents and an uncle who owned a skirt factory in Cortland, New York. He left college for a job as a brakeman, but in early 1905, at the age of twenty-two, moved to Cortland to work for his uncle. At the factory he had met Grace Brown, and there then occurred the events which led to her death a year and a half later.

The significance of Dreiser's reliance upon newspaper accounts of the Gillette trial both while in California and later in New York is that these journalistic sources, unlike the trial record, supplied a suggestive outline of Gillette's early life. Dreiser was immediately at home with this material in several important ways, and his decision to stop work on *The Bulwark* and undertake *An American Tragedy* can be attributed not only to the doldrums he was experiencing with the first but also to the excitement generated in him by the autobiographical potential of the second. For over five years Dreiser had been plumbing his memory for *A Hoosier Holiday* (1916) and for the unpublished but completed *Dawn* and *A Book about Myself*. He found, therefore, that the similarity of his own background to Gillette's provided not only an immediately available base of autobiographical detail and incident for fictional use, but also a vital emotional identification with his protagonist which was a necessary stimulus for Dreiser in the undertaking of any lengthy project. He thus began *An American Tragedy* with an uncharacteristically full account of the early life of his central figure. All his other completed novels had begun either with their protagonists in their later teens (*Sister Carrie* and *Jennie Gerhardt*) or with brief sketches of their youth (*The "Genius"* and *The Financier*). Given this tendency and given the fact that the great bulk of Dreiser's available source material dealt with Gillette's Cortland activities, he would have been expected to have begun *An American Tragedy* with Clyde's arrival in Lycurgus (as he had begun *Sister Carrie* with Carrie's arrival in Chicago). Instead, Dreiser's twenty-chapter first draft of *An American Tragedy* has the autobiographical completeness of *Dawn*. It begins long before Clyde's birth with several chapters on his parents' background, and it concludes with Clyde still only in his midteens. Although Dreiser in later versions of the novel was to compress this chronology and to omit much explicit autobiographical incident, he was still to base the central themes of book 1 of *An American Tragedy* on what can be called his autobiographical imagination.

The distinctive shape that Dreiser gave his identification with Gillette in *An American Tragedy* can best be described in connection with the prologuelike opening vignette in the novel, a vignette which is present in the first and all subsequent drafts of the work. The scene of the reluctant twelve year old accompanying his parents on a street-preaching mission while around him looms a desirable yet walled city expresses in one image of thwarted desire both the full range of Dreiser's youthful experience and his ability to project that experience into the circumstances of Gillette's life. As characterized in newspaper stories, Mr. Gillette was a nebulous and ineffectual figure, while Mrs. Gillette was the unworldly but resolute mainstay of the family. Dreiser reinforced these accounts with his recollection of a fuzzy-minded real estate man named Asa Conklin and his strong-willed wife for whom he had worked in Chicago and his more recent impressions of a fanatically religious Los Angeles couple who were his landlords during the early portion of his stay in Los Angeles. But underlying these sources was Dreiser's memory of the immense handicap imposed upon him by his own "peculiarly nebulous, emotional, unorganized and traditionless" family, and in particular his memory of a father whose primitive religiosity made him incapable of fighting the battle of life and of a mother who was the stalwart emotional center of the family.

The Clyde who so hesitantly accompanies his parents in this opening scene derives loosely from Dreiser's knowledge that Gillette escaped from his parents' control at fourteen and that he was later attracted by socially prominent girls at Cortland. Gillette as one encounters him in all the sources available to Dreiser was a callous and shallow youth who undoubtedly murdered Grace Brown. The Clyde of the first draft of *An American Tragedy*, however, is primarily the "poetic" and "romantic" but ineffectual seeker of beauty who dominates Dreiser's self-characterization in *Dawn*. He is a youth "unduly responsive to the moods as well as the lures of life, speculative and meditative and yet with no great resources of either skill or subtlety in handling the material problems of life." Like Dreiser's, his aspirations have been shaped by the American myth of success into a configuration in which sex and material splendor unite in the image of a beautiful and wealthy young girl. Clyde as a boy recalls stories in which "by reason of accidental contact with and marriage to some rich and beautiful girl, some youth no better than himself indeed had come into complete control of all her wealth. Verily. The papers said so." In his daydreams, "always he was some fabulously wealthy man's or woman's adopted son and heir, or the husband or lover of some marvellously beautiful and wealthy girl who was indulging him in every luxury."

Thus, the two poles of Clyde's emotional life in the vignette — the limiting and embarrassing world of his family and the desirable and implicitly sexual and luxurious world of the city — are a distillation of the pain and frustration of Dreiser the outsider as depicted in *Dawn* and *A Hoosier Holiday*. More particularly, Dreiser later drew upon the specific circumstances which he associated with these emotional realities to create such major incidents in book 1 as Esta's pregnancy and Clyde's work at the Green-Davidson. Gillette had in his background neither a pregnancy of this kind nor an association with a hotel. Dreiser, however, had been acutely troubled during his Warsaw years by the socially embarrassing affairs and pregnancies of his sisters. And as a young reporter in St. Louis he had delighted in the bustle and splendor of fashionable hotels and in the exciting freedom of bohemian restaurants.

But though the first draft of *An American Tragedy* which Dreiser wrote in California during 1920–21 begins with this powerfully evocative vignette, it is on the whole dull and formless. After the opening street scene, Dreiser goes back in time to recount at considerable length the early life of Asa and Elvira on New York farms, their engagement, marriage, and financial hardships, and their years in Chicago, Omaha, and Kansas City as evangelists. At chapter 7 he turns to Clyde, who is then seven. We learn of Clyde's difficulties at school because of his family and — for several chapters — of his experiences as an employee in a five-and-ten-cent store. Chapters 12–15 continue to tell of Clyde's Kansas City life but also include accounts of Esta's seduction and pregnancy and of the decision of the Gillette family to move to Denver because of Esta. In Denver, Clyde gets a job as a stock clerk in a wholesale grocery, and the draft ends with an extended narrative of his duties and problems as a clerk.

One reason for the failure of this early version of Clyde's youth is Dreiser's paradoxical overdevelopment of the few specific details about Gillette's background which were at his disposal. For example, he knew from the newspaper accounts of the Gillettes not only that Mr. Gillette was fuzzy-minded and Mrs. Gillette a rough bulwark of strength, but that the family had been footloose during Chester's boyhood and that they had been followers for several years of the Reverend John Dowie, a faith healer who had established a community called the City of Zion near Chicago in the late 1890s. In the first draft, Dreiser dramatized these details literally and fully.

As a result the draft has a static shapelessness, since Dreiser takes nineteen chapters to establish repetitiously themes implicit in the street-scene vignette of the opening chapter. To sense the prolixity and formlessness of the original version of *An American Tragedy,* one has only to contrast the splendid economy of book 1 of the final version, in which we move swiftly from the opening vignette to the contrasting motifs of Esta's pregnancy and Clyde's job in the soda fountain.

Dreiser was also overcommitted in this first draft to specific auto-biographical incidents as a means of expressing the themes he associated with his own youth. Although Dreiser no doubt intended in the long run to have Clyde work in a Green-Davidson kind of hotel in Denver, he nevertheless also thought it necessary to take him through a series of early jobs, each of which was loosely or explicitly based on an experience of Dreiser's own adolescence.

A final kind of literal-mindedness in the early version of *An American Tragedy* was Dreiser's overexplicit reliance on the Freudian and behavioristic ideas which had absorbed him during the half-decade or so before he began writing the novel. Freud's ideas had become known among American intellectuals and bohemians about 1910, and Dreiser almost immediately reflected this currency by a reference in *The Financier* to Cowperwood's "super-self." Dreiser himself, however, dated his full awareness of Freudian psychology from approximately mid-1914, when he settled in Greenwich Village. By 1917 he had accepted many of Freud's ideas and was anxious to meet his foremost American disciple and translator, A. A. Brill. Freud, he wrote Brill in early 1919, after reading one of his translations, "is like a master with a key who unlocks subterranean cells and leads forth the hoary victims of injustice." Dreiser was also an enthusiastic believer during these years in the theories of Jacques Loeb and in the behavioristic ideas of such followers of Loeb as George Crile. Loeb first came into national prominence in 1912 with his *The Mechanistic Conception of Life.* Dreiser became absorbed in his ideas a few years later at about the same time he was growing enthusiastic about Freudianism. "Mechanism plus behaviorism . . . had seized upon me," he recalled of his Village years before his departure for California.

On the surface, it would seem that Freudianism and mechanism are antithetical, and, indeed, there was much hostility between followers of the two beliefs. While Freud viewed man as unique because of his repression of his instinctive emotions—a quality which results in the dark and impenetrable undergrowth of the unconscious—Loeb stressed that all life, including man, could be observed and explained as a tropistic response to external stimuli. One school sought complexity in the explanation of human nature, the other a reductive simplicity. Both, however, viewed human behavior as deterministically controlled. Man's actions, whether the product of the unconscious or of external stimuli, were conditioned by his biological makeup and his environment. It was thus not difficult for Dreiser to accept both theories and to combine their deterministic themes in the term "chemism"—a term which he began using in 1915 or 1916 and which, as Ellen Moers has shown, he derived from Freud but used principally with a mechanistic intent. And it was inevitable, given Dreiser's penchant for intellectualizing his literary work, that these ideas should figure prominently in his writing of this period.

So Dreiser in *The Hand of the Potter* (1918), a play which he subtitled "A Tragedy," portrayed sympathetically a youthful sex maniac whose chemical makeup is the source of his behavior. So, too, the essays of *Hey Rub-a-Dub-Dub* (1920) play alternately on the beliefs of Loeb and Freud in order to help establish the major theme of the book—that the "constant palaver" about man's moral nature is indeed only talk and that the only "morality" in life is a mechanistic equation or balance.

Dreiser's twofold use of the ideas of Freud and Loeb—to defend those who are accused of "immorality" and to attack those who view life in moral terms—became increasingly strident during his last years in New York and his early stay in Los Angeles. For example, in his *Gallery of Women* sketches (written for the most part during the early 1920s), he analyzed such figures as Lucia, Emanuela, and Ernita as Freudian case studies. And in his story "Her Boy" he sharpened his earlier vague idea of "temperament" as the source of human motivation into an explicit Loebian behaviorism. "We think" he wrote in extenuation of Eddie Meagher, "that we act according to definite rules and judgments of our own or of others, but invariably, at each period we act only according to our internal chemical lures and attractions and compulsions and the outward pressures by which these same are surrounded."

The first draft of *An American Tragedy* has much of this doctrinaire quality. Esta is not only a "moony" and naive adolescent but also the product of a particular chemical formulation. A minor figure, such as Clyde's Kansas City friend Teget (dropped entirely from later versions of the novel), is displayed as a mechanism. Teget is a boy with a wanderlust, but to Dreiser, "by reason of some tropism of his nature, [he] was all for travel." It is Clyde above all who suffers the full burden of Dreiser's preoccupation with man as a biological formula. In an unpublished essay of 1918 or 1919 called "It" ("it" is man's Freudian unconscious), Dreiser wrote: "The Freudians would have us believe . . . that even the so-called temperamental leanings which influence us to take up our various professions or labors are accidental, due to psychic wounds in infancy or youth, repressions or woes, which burst out later in retaliatory decision and works." In the first draft of *An American Tragedy*, Dreiser interpreted Clyde as a figure controlled by a psychic wound, and he apparently intended to make this interpretation central to his depiction of Clyde in the novel as a whole. While still attending school in Kansas City, Clyde lies to his classmates about his parents because he is embarrassed to admit that they are street preachers. His lies lead to a confrontation with several boys, one of whom strikes Clyde, who in his fear and chagrin does not fight back. The incident, Dreiser tells us, was important because

> a deep psychic wound had been delivered which was destined to fester and ramify in strange ways later on. It convinced him of the material, even the spiritual insignificance of that which his parents did. They seemed, if anything, more hopeless and incompetent than ever. It sickened him of this school, and this type of school work, as well as of the type of prosperous youth of better physique perhaps who could thus bluster and brag and insult and show off. At the same time, and by some psychic process of inversion, it gave him a greater awe of wealth and comfort, or at least a keener perception of the protective quality of a high social position in life.

The final version of *An American Tragedy* still bears the marks of Dreiser's intense interest in mechanistic and Freudian ideas. Esta's adolescent mooniness is still a "chemism of dreams" and Mason, later in the novel, is briefly characterized in relation to a "psychic sex scar" which is the product of his boyhood experiences. But on the whole Dreiser was able to free the novel in later drafts from straitjacket formulistic characterizations by assimilating his Freudian and behavioristic beliefs into independently realized dramatic moments and psychological responses.

All signs indicate that Dreiser completed the twenty extant chapters of his first draft in early 1921 and that he then put aside the novel. Perhaps he felt the need to view the area in which most of the later action of the novel was to take place. But also, as is suggested by his having stopped work long before he reached the Lycurgus portion and by his later almost complete discarding of the draft, he was consciously or unconsciously dissatisfied with his overliteral, overpolemical technique and had therefore reached a temporary dead end. Dreiser returned to New York in October 1922. Although he may have done some additional research on the Gillette case during the next nine months, he did no writing. Liveright, however, was putting increasing pressure on him to deliver the novel which was to be the cornerstone of their new and elaborate publishing agreement. So in June 1923, Dreiser and Helen made a motor trip in which they visited Cortland, South Otselic (the Biltz of *An American Tragedy*), Herkimer (Bridgeburg), and Big Moose Lake (Big Bittern Lake). On their return, Dreiser began a new draft of *An American Tragedy*. He completed all work on the novel, some million words later, in late 1925.

When Dreiser began work on his new version of *An American Tragedy* in the summer of 1923, he had available as documentary sources the extensive reports of the trial and execution of Gillette in the *New York World* and a small pamphlet called *Grace Brown's Love Letters* which contained the letters of Grace Brown to Gillette in the early summer of 1906, shortly before her death. In addition, he had visited the towns and countryside which figure in the case, and he would soon make journeys to an upper New York state shirt factory and to Sing Sing prison. The principal questions about Dreiser's use of his sources are: to what extent did he depend on the verbatim trial record of the case as well as the *World*, and to what extent does his account of the life of Clyde Griffiths after his arrival at Lycurgus differ from the account in his sources of Gillette at Cortland. Both matters are important, since the first bears on the shaping influence of a particular source and the second on the distinctive themes and form which Dreiser imposed upon his sources.

Although Dreiser had asked to see the trial record of the Gillette case in August 1920, and though the record would have been available to him in New York City on his return in 1922, there is no evidence that he indeed ever did consult it. Dreiser seldom discussed the explicit sources he used for the novel, and his fullest statement on this matter is ambiguous. He wrote in 1935 in "I Find the Real American Tragedy,"

> Furthermore, in my examination of such data as I could find in 1924 relating to the Chester Gillette-Billy Brown case, I had become convinced that there was an entire misunderstanding, or perhaps I had better say non-apprehension, of the conditions or circumstances surrounding the victims of that murder *before* the murder was committed. From these circumstances, which I drew not only from the testimony introduced at the trial but from newspaper investigations and information which preceded and accompanied the trial. . . .

The key phrase in this recollection — "the testimony introduced at the trial" — would seem to refer to the trial record but for the fact that the *World* published much purportedly verbatim testimony and that a comparison of *An American*

Tragedy, the *World,* and the Gillette trial record reveals that Dreiser depended exclusively on the *World* for his verbatim material and for almost all other explicit detail.

The *World* reporter did not take exact notes but rather paraphrased loosely and then placed this material in quotation marks as if he were quoting directly. All of Dreiser's verbatim use of material from the trial follows the *World*'s version rather than the trial record, as can be seen from this comparison of the opening of the district attorney's speech to the jury at the beginning of the trial:

Trial Record	*New York World*	*An American Tragedy*
"You probably, those of you who are unfamiliar with the process of selecting a jury, have marvelled somewhat during the past week as the attorneys for the defense and the People have exercised those rights which the law gives to them in selecting a jury."	"No doubt many of you have been puzzled during the past week by the care with which the lawyers in the case have passed upon the panels from which you twelve men have been drawn."	"No doubt many of you have been wearied, as well as puzzled, at times during the past week," he began, "by the exceeding care with which the lawyers in this case have passed upon the panels from which you twelve men have been chosen."

Dreiser's dramatization of Clyde's life in Lycurgus, including the trip to the North Woods with Roberta, is equally conclusive in indicating the *World* as Dreiser's major source. He used a great mass of detail which is present only in the *World,* while conversely, with a few possible exceptions, he did not use any detail which is present only in the trial record.

The appeal of the *World* to Dreiser as the principal source of his knowledge of the Gillette case is readily explainable. The printed trial record comprises over 2000 pages of testimony, much of it involving the selection of a jury, extensive medical evidence, and the full examination and cross-examination of minor witnesses. The account in the *World* summarized such matters in favor of a full coverage of sensational evidence and emotional moments in the trial and much material on such vital concerns for a novelist as Gillette's background, his Cortland love affairs, the atmosphere in the court, the appearance and actions of participants in the trial, and the circumstances of

Gillette's execution. Thus, for example, it was from the *World*'s emphasis on the formal addresses of the attorneys and on Gillette's testimony that Dreiser derived his own summary version of the trial, and it was from the *World* that he received the hint that Grace Brown had a single major rival for the affections of Gillette. The *World*, in short, supplied a good deal of grist for the novelist's mill not available elsewhere and gave this material, by means of emphasis and selection, a kind of preliminary fictional expression which Dreiser had the good sense to recognize as invaluable.

The nature and extent of Dreiser's use of the *World* reports of the Gillette trial are important because of the myth that *An American Tragedy* is merely a slightly fictionalized version of the case. In fact, Dreiser relied on the Gillette case but was not bound by it. His intent was not to retell a story but to recast Gillette's experience into an American tragedy — that is, into a story which would render the tragic reality at the center of the American dream. He therefore made a large number of changes from his sources, all of which are related to two basic impulses: to shift the unavoidable impression of the documentary evidence that Gillette was a shallowminded murderer to the impression that Clyde might be any one of us caught in the insoluble conflict between our deepest needs and the unyielding nature of experience; and to transform the shapeless, repetitious, and superficial manifestation of life in an actual trial into the compelling revelation of human nature and experience present in fiction at its best. Dreiser's changes were therefore not so much those of addition or omission as of reinterpreting and reshaping what was available to him.

The events of the Gillette case occurred in Cortland, Big Moose Lake, and Herkimer from early 1905 to the summer of 1906. Dreiser made two significant changes in this setting: he moved Clyde's Lycurgus experience forward into the post-World War I period, and he changed the location of Cortland and Herkimer.

With some exceptions which I shall note later, Dreiser followed the chronology of his sources in his account of Clyde's arrival in Lycurgus in the early spring, his courting first of Roberta and then of Sondra that summer, fall, and winter, his expedition to the Adirondack lakes with Roberta the following summer, his trial that same fall, and his electrocution a year and a half after his trial. Yet he sets this sequence of events vaguely in the early 1920s rather than in 1905–8. Vaguely, because Dreiser does not mention a specific date or historical event in the entire novel. Rather, he depends on the prevalence and importance in the novel of automobiles, of references to movies and popular music, and of an ambience of dancing and prohibition-style parties to establish a sense of the twenties. An indication of the specific period Dreiser had in mind is revealed by his statement both in the holograph and in an early typescript of book 2 that Clyde arrives in Lycurgus in 1919.

Dreiser moved the "present" of the novel forward into the contemporary because he wished to enforce the theme that America, for all its postwar "freedom" and even license, was still a nation in which the combination of the immense attraction of wealth and a pervasive moral hypocrisy could cause the destruction of a Clyde Griffiths. His intent, in other words, was to stress the continuity of American experience. When Dreiser read in the *World* that during a Sunday break in the Gillette trial, "the jury went in a body today to services at the Methodist church," he saw reflected the present of the 1920s as well as the past of 1906 and of his own boyhood. The "tragedy" of the Dreiser family in various small Indiana towns of the 1880s was still the American tragedy. Youthful desire and need were still fed the illusion of hope and were still blighted by the reality of blocked opportunities and a stifling moralism. As Dreiser wrote in an article of early 1921, "I can truthfully say that I can not detect, in the post-war activities or interests, social, intellectual or otherwise, of the younger or other generations of Americans, poor, rich, or middle class, any least indication of the breaking of hampering shackles of any kind — intellectual, social, monetary, or what you will."

Dreiser was correct in his view of the twenties, for the myth of that decade as a period of freedom rests largely on Jazz Age writing of revolt and rebellion, of writing which is consciously opposed to such middle-class American beliefs and values as those expressed in the symbols of the Small Town, the Middle West, and Business. Acts of rebellion, whether in art or life, imply a powerful though sometimes inarticulate cultural base against which revolt takes shape and seeks expression. *An American Tragedy* is thus a novel of the twenties not so much in its external trappings as in the relationship of some of Dreiser's basic themes to the major fiction of revolt of the period. Like Hemingway, Lewis, and Fitzgerald, Dreiser depicts the falseness and destructiveness of such American illusions as the faith in moral abstractions, the implicit virtue of small-town or rural life, and the association of one's noblest dreams with a wealthy girl.

Dreiser's changes in the interior chronology of the Gillette case are of interest, but only two require discussion. He revised the date of Roberta's pregnancy from late March to early February in order to prolong and intensify the pressure on Clyde before the death trip and to make possible his several abortion attempts. And he shifted the three-week-long trial backward from its opening date of November 13 to October 15. His purpose was to intensify a theme which had its origin in the Herkimer County political scene at the time of the Gillette trial. Both A. M. Mills and Charles D. Thomas, Gillette's two court-appointed lawyers, were political enemies of George W. Ward, the prosecuting district attorney. On November 5, before the trial began, Ward had run for county judge on the Republican ticket and had won, while Thomas had run for state senator as a Democrat and had lost. This political rivalry then spilled over into the trial and was frequently commented upon by the *World,* including a remark that Ward had won in a closely fought contest primarily because of a campaign promise to prosecute Gillette vigorously. In order to add strength to the theme that justice is often a contest in which the strong climb to success upon the backs of the weak, Dreiser moved the trial back almost a month and also made Belknap (one of Clyde's lawyers) and Mason (the district attorney) rivals for the same office. Thus, Mason is in a sense campaigning in court and the conviction of Clyde guarantees his victory.

Dreiser also changed the location of Cortland and Herkimer, the Lycurgus and Bridgeburg of *An American Tragedy.* Cortland, which is approximately thirty miles directly south of Syracuse, is in a comparatively poor and sparsely populated area of central New York. When Dreiser saw it in 1923, it had about 15,000 inhabitants. Dreiser's decision to increase its size and move it to a more prosperous and thickly settled area stemmed from his tendency in the use of his sources to widen the social and financial distance between Clyde and the Griffithses in order to strengthen the theme that Clyde's hopes are illusions. The Griffithses of Lycurgus are considerably more wealthy and socially prominent than were the Gillettes of Cortland, and Clyde is far more distant from their world initially than Chester Gillette had been from the Gillettes'. For many of these changes, as well as for the thematically important portrayal of the lively younger set of Lycurgus, with their exciting parties in neighboring cities, he needed a town which was larger than Cortland and which was located in a more prosperous and populous section. He therefore moved Cortland some 100 miles east into the area of large manufacturing cities at the confluence of the Mohawk and the Hudson, and he more than doubled its size.

Herkimer, the county seat where Gillette was tried, is near Utica on the southern edge of Herkimer County, which stretches about 100 miles from the far North Woods to the bustling Mohawk Valley. Dreiser moved Cataraqui County, his version of Herkimer County, further north and shortened its length to fifty miles. The effect of this change is to make Bridgeburg, the county seat where Clyde is tried, a North Woods village and thereby to increase sharply the potential for portraying the narrowness and the pressures for conformity of village morality. Thus, Dreiser made Lycurgus more cosmopolitan than Cortland and Bridgeburg more rural than Herkimer.

Dreiser's most important changes, however, involve the participants and events of the Gillette case. His transformation of Gillette into Clyde was informed by two fundamental purposes. He wanted to give Clyde a powerful motive for the death of Roberta other than her pregnancy, and he wanted to cast doubt on the certainty that her death was a murder. Both of these desires led to considerable variation from his sources. In order to intensify and sharpen Clyde's motive, Dreiser lowered Gillette's social position, made his romance with Grace Brown a greater threat to his social aspirations, and supplied him with a second love who promised both wealth and position. Gillette had attended college, was readily accepted into "what passed for high society in Cortland" (Ellen Moers's phrase), and did not attempt to hide his affair with Grace Brown. In addition, though the *World* singled out Hattie Benedict, the daughter of a Cortland lawyer, as the most important of Gillette's interests among "the younger set" of the town, Gillette in fact played the field and had no single all-consuming passion similar to that of Clyde for Sondra. Given Gillette's circumstances in Lycurgus, it is no wonder that his murder of Grace Brown appears to be incredibly stupid and callous and that one of the principal defenses adopted by his attorneys was the lack of motive. Clyde, however, because he believes he can murder Roberta without detection and because of his overpowering desire to gain the kind of life represented by Sondra, is endowed with a motive which helps create the powerful psychological and narrative tension of book 2.

The most damaging piece of circumstantial evidence against Gillette, in a case based entirely on such evidence since there were no eyewitnesses, was the tennis racket with which he supposedly struck Grace Brown. Gillette had left his suitcase and camera on shore while he and Grace Brown were on Big Moose together but had taken the racket with him. After her death, he had hidden the racket on shore. The battered and broken racket and Grace Brown's extensive head wounds strongly supported the contention of the state that Gillette, with premeditation, had first knocked Grace into the water with a blow to the face and had then struck her on the head with the racket until she sank. On his arrest, Gillette had explained that Grace fell into the water accidentally, though he offered at different times three varying versions of the accident. At the trial, however, his defense was that he told Grace while they were in the boat that her only recourse was to tell her parents about her pregnancy. She thereupon had stood up suddenly, had said "You don't know my father. . . . I'll end it all now," and had tipped over the boat. She had already sunk, Gillette claimed, when he himself came to the surface.

Dreiser changed both the "facts" of Grace Brown's death and Gillette's "lie" about her death. He omitted entirely the tennis racket as a possible weapon and substituted for it a camera, an object which Clyde not only might legitimately take with him on the boat (thus making the case for the defense more plausible) but also one with which he could have struck Roberta accidentally (thus introducing the moral ambiguity of her death, a theme entirely lacking in the Gillette case). Dreiser's intent in this crucial change was to make Clyde much less obviously and conclusively guilty of murder both in our view, as "eyewitnesses" of Roberta's death, and in the view of the jury as it weighs the circumstantial evidence surrounding her death. So, too, he made Roberta's wounds much less severe than Grace's, and so, too, he omitted such clearly implausible testimony as Gillette's claim that he still loved Grace at the time of her death.

Dreiser's change of the "lie" about Roberta's death did not stem from his desire to make Clyde more sympathetic than Gillette in this particular instance. Both Gillette's account of Grace Brown's suicide and Clyde's change-of-heart story are patently false and self-serving. Rather he wished to substitute a thematically functional lie for one which was thematically inefficient. The lie which Clyde's lawyer Jephson prepares in order to explain the events in the boat is deeply and powerfully ironic in relation to Dreiser's reconstruction of Grace's death. For Clyde indeed did have a "change of heart," though of courage rather than of intent. And his recasting of that change into a "moral" decision for the benefit of the jury is so unconvincing that it in fact weakens rather than strengthens his case.

Of course, these and similar changes in the circumstances of Grace Brown's death and in Gillette's explanation of it are but the external signs of Dreiser's transformation of the superficial reality of the Gillette he knew into the psychological reality which is Clyde. It is a transformation which stems from the novelist's ability to take the faceless surface of experience — the testimony at a trial — and to create from it an inner life which, as Clyde sits transfixed in the boat while Roberta crawls toward him, we know fully and therefore compassionately. Dreiser's changes thus explain only the direction of his transformation; they do not explain the power of the novel.

Dreiser's knowledge of Grace Brown derived from testimony about her and from her love letters to Gillette, which were read in full at the trial by District Attorney Ward and then published in pamphlet form. Her letters are indeed moving, for they have the natural eloquence of a direct statement of need and heartbreak. The Grace Brown who emerges from the testimony, from her letters, and from Ward's constant reference to her as a "plucked flower" or its equivalent, is above all a pathetic figure. Dreiser was, of course, conscious of the pathos of the discarded woman and in particular the pathos of the pregnant lower-class girl who has nowhere to turn. Indeed, he created one of the most moving scenes in the novel — Roberta's interview with the doctor who refuses her an abortion — out of the experiences of his sisters Mame and Sylvia. But he was also aware that a pathetic situation could arouse strength and resiliency in women, as in the strong-willed self-righteousness of Sallie and the intuitive selfishness of Mame at crises in their lives. He therefore maintained the pathos of Roberta's dilemma but also shaped her character into a far more complex and credible reality than the paragon of rural innocence who is the Grace Brown of the Gillette trial. Roberta's self-pity has both a soft and a hard edge during her later relations with Clyde; she not only begs but demands that Clyde "do right" by her. And her rural innocence is also a confining moralism which links sex irrevocably with marriage, a state of mind which Dreiser associated especially with Sallie.

District Attorney Ward referred both in his opening and closing speeches to Gillette's interest in socially prominent girls but was unable to prove a single dominant flirtation. The *World,* however, described Hattie Benedict as "the Cortland girl with whom Gillette is said to have fallen in love shortly before Grace Brown's death" and as the girl who "supplanted Grace Brown in Gillette's affection." Miss Benedict testified briefly at the trial (the Gillette trial contained no "Miss X" agreement), as did a number of other girls of her set in whom Gillette had shown an interest. But she merely stated that she and Gillette had spent July 4 at York Lake, near Cortland, and that Gillette was only an acquaintance.

Dreiser seized upon the prominence given Miss Benedict in the *World* to create the figure of Sondra. Aside from Clyde's early and brief flirtation with Rita, his love affairs at Lycurgus are confined to Roberta and Sondra, unlike Gillette's wide-ranging activities. Dreiser's centering of all of Clyde's desires and dreams on the charismatic figure of Sondra was perhaps his most important imaginative act in his recasting of Gillette's life at Cortland, for the substitution of a single compelling interest for a general preference for socially prominent girls is the difference between the shapelessness of fact and the form of fiction. Dreiser followed broadly the outline suggested by the Gillette case in his account of Clyde's relationship to the Lycurgus Griffithses, to the factory, and to Roberta. But his account of Clyde's association with Sondra — her background and character, his courting of her, and the nature and intensity of his interest in her — was entirely "invented." And those facts of the case which conflicted with this "invented" material were suppressed or recast. For example, while Gillette and Grace Brown were traveling in separate railway cars on their way to Utica and then to the North Woods, Gillette met two upper-class Cortland girls whom he knew and made a date to go camping with them at Seventh Lake a few days later. After murdering Grace, he indeed did meet the two girls and go on a camping trip with them, and he was arrested at a Fourth Lake hotel three days after the murder. Dreiser substituted for his casual date with the two Cortland girls Clyde's prearranged plan to join Sondra at Twelfth Lake. He thus changed Gillette's casual flirting to Clyde's tortured last days with Sondra, days in which his prize is near and yet is also receding rapidly as Mason approaches.

Almost all the action and minor characters of Clyde's life in Lycurgus are briefly sketched in Dreiser's sources or derive from the ability of the novelist to fill in vaguely introduced social realities, such as a family or a factory or a boardinghouse, with specific characters and events. Dreiser handles this thinly suggested material with great freedom in order to shape theme and form out of the flotsam and jetsam of experience. To cite an obvious example, Harold Gillette, Chester's cousin, is mentioned briefly in Dreiser's sources as a twenty-one-year-old superintendent in the factory who warned Chester that it was unwise to continue seeing Grace Brown. From these spare details, Dreiser created the major theme of Gilbert Griffiths as Clyde's double in physical appearance but his unreachable superior in class, wealth, and intellect. He spun out from this theme one thread of plot involving Gilbert's resentment against both Clyde and Sondra because they represent threats to his position at the factory and in local society and another thread involving Sondra's cultivation of Clyde in order to pique Gilbert. Another example is Gillette's two lawyers, Mills and Thomas. They are not sharply differentiated in Dreiser's sources except that Mills is considerably older than Thomas and is the senior counsel for the defense. But Dreiser, seizing upon the opportunity to create significant distinction where there are two of anything, shapes Belknap (Mills) into a worldly man of experience who sympathizes with Clyde, and Jephson (Thomas) into a brilliant young man who sees the case primarily as a challenge to his will and intellect.

Dreiser's use of the Gillette case also involved a recasting of his source from its form as evidence and commentary within a trial lasting three weeks into a narrative of a year and a half in Clyde's life. His basic method was to dramatize as a single sequence of action antedating the trial most of the repetitious detail presented in the trial which bears on Gillette's life in Lycurgus and to compress and reorganize the events of the trial itself in order to emphasize the thematically significant and the dramatic.

The Gillette trial, like most trials, was exceedingly tedious for the most part, even as reported in the *World* in condensed form and with the highlighting of sensational journalism. It took five days to select a jury, over a hundred witnesses were examined and cross-examined, and the largest single body of evidence involved technical medical details. By loosely following the

World's pattern of summary and emphasis but by imposing on the material in the *World* a further selectivity and a fuller dramatization of key moments, Dreiser turned reportage into fiction. Thus, Dreiser devotes only a few sentences to the selection of a jury, and he summarizes briefly the medical testimony and the testimony of minor witnesses. (Indeed, he presents in testimony format only two witnesses other than Gillette.) On the other hand, he presents in great detail the courtroom atmosphere, the opening speeches of the prosecution and defense attorneys, and the examination and cross-examination of Clyde.

Dreiser begins his dramatization of the trial with a version of Ward's speech. By omitting most of Ward's lengthy account of the death trip and by introducing some of Ward's remarks from his closing summation speech, he underlined Mason's appeal to the sexual and moral prejudices of his audience. Dreiser then summarized the evidence offered by the state, stressing such sensational details emphasized by the *World* as the undeveloped pictures found in Gillette's camera and the "death scream" heard by a woman tourist on the lake. He concluded the state's case with Mason reading passages from Roberta's letters to Clyde. Clyde's defense, like Gillette's, consists almost entirely of his attorney's opening address and his own testimony. But Dreiser revised this material in several significant ways. He lengthened Belknap's opening speech, including in it material from Mills's closing speech in order to stress several themes that otherwise were weak or diffuse in the original defense — that Clyde was a "moral and mental coward," that he should not be convicted of murder merely because he wished to desert his pregnant sweetheart, and that the jury should weigh heavily the overpowering temptation provided by Miss X. Dreiser then expanded Clyde's direct examination to include much information on his youth and his relationship to Miss X which was not present in the direct examination of Gillette. The bulk of Clyde's direct examination is thus devoted to the most sympathetic side of his character — his boyhood deprivations and his intolerable position when he found himself caught between the demands of Roberta and the dream of Sondra. Unlike Gillette's direct examination, which was largely an implausible explanation of the events of the death trip, Clyde's is a moving plea for recognition of his dilemma.

Clyde's cross-examination by Mason, lengthy as it is, is brief compared to the two days which Ward took to cross-examine Gillette. Dreiser preserved Ward's technique of moving rapidly from topic to topic (adopted, the *World* noted, to rattle Gillette) as well as Ward's attack on the contradictions and implausibilities in Gillette's story — the false names used on the trip, the suitcase left on shore, the failure to ask the price of the boat, the incriminating map of the Big Moose area, and so on. But he used verbatim very little of Ward's repetitious and often inept cross-examination (he had not used verbatim any of Mills's direct examination of Gillette), and he rearranged and made more emphatic the substance of Ward's attack on the credibility of Gillette's story. In short, he made Mason a more effective trial attorney than Ward.

Throughout the trial as recreated by Dreiser, the courtroom audience is a living presence. From hints in the *World* about the intense community antagonism against Gillette—at one time the judge was reported to be prepared to ask for state militia to prevent a lynching—and from a report on the nature of the jury's deliberations he created a felt presence of mass hate which colors Clyde's fate from the moment he walks for the first time through the hostile crowd on his way from the jail to the courtroom until the single juror holding out against conviction is cowed and threatened into submission by his angry fellow jurors.

Dreiser's recasting of the trial was thus not only in the direction of compression and dramatic representation but also toward the theme that the complexities and needs of human nature are usually submerged and overcome by the certainties of group prejudice. He thus shifted our attention as observers of the trial from the "logic" of the mass of evidence against Gillette—in particular the medical evidence—to the principal extenuating circumstance in Clyde's actions, the meaning of Miss X in his life. We are moved to ponder not the blow on the head which was the immediate cause of Roberta's death, but the underlying cause—the emotional reality of Miss X.

Dreiser's use of Grace Brown's love letters offers the best single example of his shaping of documentary material into fictional reality and of his recasting of the trial as reported into the trial as depicted. Grace Brown wrote fourteen love letters, two in April during a brief visit to South Otselic and the remainder during June and July, while she waited in South Otselic for Gillette to take some action about her pregnancy. Ward arranged the state's presentation of evidence in strict chronological sequence. He therefore read all the letters to the jury early in the case—that is, before the extensive evidence concerning the death trip.

Dreiser's first major adaptation of this material was to move four of the longest and most crucial letters from the trial to the dramatic action of the period just before the trip to the North Woods. In these letters, Roberta's tone changes from loneliness and anxiety to threats as she begins to fear that Clyde will remain inactive if he can. In the trial itself, Dreiser rearranged the order of the state's case. Instead of reading the letters early in his presentation, Mason saves them until the close and then reads only six of the most pathetic passages in order to enforce emotionally his implied contention that

Clyde deserves to die for mistreating and deserting his pregnant sweetheart whether or not he actually murdered her. Both in the letters used before the trial and in those read during the trial, Dreiser mixed verbatim quotation, loose paraphrase, and new material—yet maintained the emotional texture of alternating pleading and recrimination, and hope and fear, of the original letters.

The extent of Dreiser's verbatim use of Grace Brown's letters is exemplified by the four letters he worked into the narrative of Clyde's life in Lycurgus. Of these, one is almost entirely verbatim; one is heavily verbatim; one—the longest—is loosely paraphrased and adapted from a number of letters, with much new material as well; and one is completely new except for a single sentence. Moreover, Dreiser sharpened Grace Brown's threat to come to Cortland—presumably to plead directly with Gillette—into Roberta's explicit threat to expose Clyde to his relatives and upper-class girl friends. Dreiser therefore did rely heavily on Grace Brown's letters, often with a verbatim exactness. But he also rearranged the letters to permit them to play a more significant role both in his narrative of Clyde's life in Lycurgus and in his depiction of the trial, and he subtly intensified the heartbreak and the anger present in the originals into themes which bear directly on the characterization of Clyde and Roberta.

For Clyde in prison, Dreiser relied on the accounts in the *World* of Gillette's final days to shape a narrative in which Clyde alternated between the conflicting emotions of fear generated by the "death house," guilt arising from his lies to his mother, and hopes because of the interest which the Reverend McMillan shows in his fate. Mrs. Griffiths's activities in book 3 were based closely on those of Mrs. Gillette in the interval between Gillette's sentencing and his execution. McMillan has a distant source in the Reverend Henry MacIlravy who became Gillette's "spiritual adviser" in the weeks preceding his execution. With the aid of MacIlravy and the prison chaplain, Gillette released, just before his death, a penitent statement addressed to the youth of America that Dreiser used verbatim. And it was MacIlravy and the chaplain who stated to the press, immediately after Gillette's death, that in their view "no legal mistake was made in his electrocution." Out of these slight leads involving MacIlravy, Dreiser created the powerful and significant figure of McMillan. He also shifted the thrust of the statement concerning "no legal mistake" forward to the crucial moment in the governor's office when McMillan, because he believes that Clyde is indeed guilty, refuses to intercede on his behalf. (In fact, though Mr. and Mrs. Gillette appeared before the governor, the Reverend MacIlravy was not present at this interview.)

American Gothic: Poe and
An American Tragedy

Thomas P. Riggio

In book 2, chapter 42 of *An American Tragedy* Clyde Griffiths reads in the *Times-Union* about a girl's death by drowning in a Massachusetts lake. The incident at Pass Lake plants the idea of murder in his mind. Then, in an unusually compressed narrative sequence of six chapters, Dreiser concentrates Clyde's plunge into mental unbalance, his evolution of a murder plan, a detailed account of the events leading to the fatal act at Big Bittern Lake, and Roberta Alden's death scene. In these sixty harrowing pages Dreiser departs from the more obviously realistic mode of the novel. Ellen Moers notes that "the dream language, the complex fable-making, the phantasmagoria of Clyde's paradise world, and the gradual desubstantiation of Clyde himself all insensibly prepare us for Dreiser's Arabian Nights treatment of the murder." Dreiser achieves his special effects in these chapters through the use of a few unlikely fictive devices: a bizarre nightmare, a psychic evil genie who tempts Clyde, a gothic landscape that corresponds to his shifting perception of reality, and an equally gothic "weir-weir" bird to both herald and precipitate Clyde's murderous act. Since the novel bears evidence of Dreiser's decade-long reading in Freud and his disciples, critics naturally have looked to this source to account for the psychological import of the gothic and Arabian Nights imagery. What has not been noticed is that Dreiser's most immediate debt is not to Freud, or even directly to the *Arabian Nights*, but to the American writer who anticipated Freudian interests in inner conflicts and who employed oriental fable and gothic symbolism to analyze the mind of a murderer—Edgar Allan Poe.

From *American Literature* 49, no. 4 (January 1978). © 1978 by Duke University Press.

That Dreiser turned to Poe at a critical point in *An American Tragedy* is not surprising. He considered Poe "our first and greatest literary genius"; even "the noble Mark Twain, compromiser with convention that he was, [was] a mere clown, artistically, by the side of Poe." In June of 1921, when Dreiser was working on the first draft of the novel, he encountered Poe anew in Dr. John W. Robertson's privately printed *Poe: A Study*. A practicing psychiatrist with an appetite for literary scholarship, Dr. Robertson wrote a two-part psychological and bibliographical account of Poe which he sent to Dreiser. Dreiser's response, given in a letter to John J. Newbegin, a San Francisco book dealer, suggests the basis of Poe's appeal for him. Dreiser identified both with Poe's private pains — his "desperate attempt to escape from torturing memories" — and the public neglect he suffered in America. "I accept wholly," he wrote, "his [Dr. Robertson's] theory of morbid heredity in the case of Poe with the corollary that 'he was not always to be held responsible either for his words or acts.' He unquestionably belongs, as I have always thought, and as he makes clear, 'to that coterie of Sensitives who wear the fetters of heredity.'" Dreiser also commented on Poe's American reception as an indictment of "American letters and American critical insight," a testament to America's "horror of reality . . . the same disorder that afflicts them [Americans] today."

More to the point, however, Poe stood out for Dreiser as the one American who had mastered the techniques of portraying criminal obsessions and mental disorders. Poe provided Dreiser with models for handling a central problem of the book: how to present Roberta's death so as to retain an ambivalence about the act that would force the reader to take account of Clyde's past history, his wavering, confused mind, and the psychological factors that determine the outcome of the climactic moment on the lake. Dreiser found in Poe a writer whose work foreshadowed his own concerns with those cloudy areas where responsibility for human action blurs in the shadow-land between dream and reality, where one is the victim of unconscious drives, heredity, environment, and external stimuli. Indeed, as a concise treatment of deranged criminality, chapters 42–47 read like a Poe tale, complete with a nightmare landscape, the language of psychological analysis, and oriental and gothic trappings.

I

Immediately after reading about the accident at Pass Lake, Clyde's mind wanders to the dilemma presented by Roberta's pregnancy and Sondra Finchley's growing infatuation. The possibility of a staged accident makes its way into his consciousness. Dreiser describes the process of mind that at first attempts to repress the idea of premeditated murder.

> Still thinking of the complicated problem which his own life here presented, he was struck by the thought (what devil's whisper? — what evil hint of an evil spirit?) — supposing that he and Roberta — no, say he and Sondra — (no, Sondra could swim so well, and so could he) — he and Roberta were in a small boat somewhere and it could capsize at the very time, say, of this dreadful complication which was so harassing him? What an escape?

The syntax reflects Clyde's muddled thought, as Dreiser introduces this version of an internal voice — an evil spirit who will grow into an articulate and compelling efrit by the time Clyde makes his fated trip to Big Bittern. Such spirits eliciting the same sort of stunned self-queries, are common agents in Poe's stories of demented homicide. The narrator of "Morella," for example, contemplates the mysterious urge that leads him to baptize his child in the name of the dead Morella, thus assuring her death also: "What demon urged me to breathe that sound . . . what fiend spoke from the recesses of my soul, when amid those dim aisles, and in the silence of the night, I whispered within the ears of the holy man the syllables — Morella?" The fatal urging issues in the death of Morella's child, as Clyde's first temptation ultimately ends not only in the horror of Roberta's death but in "The death of that unborn child, too!!" Of course, Poe cast his tales in a more symbolic mold than Dreiser: the death of a secondary character often reflects the collapse of some aspect of the protagonist's mind. But Dreiser borrowed the syntax and imagery of these psychic dramas to represent, within a naturalistic framework, the workings of Clyde's subconscious mind.

Moreover, Dreiser attributes to Clyde the same temperamental and physical traits that mark mental disorder in the central figures in stories such as "The Fall of the House of Usher," "Morella," "Ligeia," and "Berenice." For example, Poe conceives the ruin of Usher's house as rooted in "the [fact that the] stem of the Usher race, all time honored as it was, had put forth, at no period, any enduring branch; in other words, that the entire family lay in the direct line of descent." Dreiser, likewise, stresses the importance of Clyde's heredity as a key to his character. He establishes early in book 1 that Clyde's family endowed him with "a kind of mental depression or melancholia which promised not so well for his future." This accounts for Clyde's "nervous esthetic inhibitions" and his most attractive characterization: his apparent "strain of refinement." Donald Pizer has noticed that " 'sensitive' is the key term in establishing the character of Clyde" (recall here the special attention Dreiser paid to Poe as one of "that coterie of Sensitives who wear the fetters of heredity") and that "Clyde's most distinctive physical characteristic [is] his 'thin and sensitive and graceful hands.'" As in Poe, however, such sensitivity does not carry positive connotations; it reflects an essential weakness of character.

Dreiser transfers these emblems of Poe's aristocratic, rarefied figures whose minds are infected by exotic, esoteric pursuits to the son of a poor "religionist" whose mind is infected by the crass, everyday glitter of a materialistic society. One trait above all marks Clyde's familial ties to Poe's world. He betrays his repressed passion, his melancholy, his fears and hatreds primarily through his eyes. Like Usher's "excessive nervous agitation," which is "above all things [centered in] the miraculous lustre of [his] eye," Clyde's inner turmoil is mirrored in his eyes: "At this point it was that a nervous and almost deranged look — never so definite or powerful at any time before in his life — the border-line between reason and unreason, no less — so powerful that the quality of it was even noticeable to Sondra — came into his eyes." In the final moments on Big Bittern, when Clyde experiences a failure of nerve, all his unarticulated passion remains centered in his eyes. It is "his eyes — the pupils of the same growing momentarily larger and more lurid" that compel Roberta toward him, thus fulfilling his murderous desire. Dreiser echoes here the words of Ligeia's lover — words Roberta might well have spoken of Clyde: "Of all the women whom I have ever known . . . Ligeia was the most violently a prey to the tumultuous vultures of stern passion. And of such passion I could form no estimate, save by the miraculous expansion of those eyes."

To explain the inner crisis Clyde's eyes betray, Dreiser begins chapter 45 not with the language of Freudian psychology but with a Poe-like preface to describe temporary insanity:

> There are moments when in connection with the sensitively imaginative or morbidly anachronistic — the mentally assailed and the same not of any great strength and the problem confronting it of sufficient force and complexity — the reason not actually toppling from its throne, still totters or is warped or shaken. . . . In such instances the will and the courage confronted by some great difficulty which it can neither master nor endure, appears in some to recede in precipitate flight, leaving only panic and temporary unreason in its wake.

Dreiser thus outlines Clyde's condition in the words Poe gives to Usher's narrator: "I fancied that I perceived, and for the first time, a full consciousness on the part of Usher of the tottering of his lofty reason upon her throne."

That Dreiser follows this imagery so closely, simply changing "tottering" to "toppling" and reserving "totters" for the next phrase, suggests the degree to which he recalled Poe as he worked on his novel. Of course, since the "fall" from sanity is meant to be only temporary, Dreiser modifies the extent of the aberration; and Clyde's reason could not in any way be called "lofty." Like Poe, Dreiser stresses the "sensitively imaginative" and morbid dimensions of his character's temperament. Clyde lacks "the will and courage" to ward off "panic and temporary unreason," as Usher's "want of moral energy"—later "moral coward" would be the verdict passed on Clyde—assures his "struggle with the grim phantasm, Fear."

With this introduction Dreiser sets the stage for Clyde's withdrawal from reality into the inner precincts of his mind. Dreiser follows Poe closely in his portrait of the dual consequences of flights from reality that convert the rational faculty into "a sealed and silent hall." Under intense strain, the mind retreats into an "inward scene" which both distorts the world of nature and dehumanizes the world of man.

Clyde's mind transforms the woodland "Paradise"—the term he uses to describe the neighboring region where Sondra spends her summers—into a gothic landscape. Dreiser anticipates this alteration of nature, as Poe so often does, through the medium of a dream. Clyde's dream in chapter 42 draws together elements from various Poe tales. Arthur Gordon Pym wakes "in a paroxysm of terror" from one nightmare only to encounter the waking terror of "white and ghastly fangs" which he later recognizes as those of his "dog Tiger." Dreiser naturally reverses the order as Clyde finds himself "dreaming of a savage black dog that was trying to bite him. Having escaped from the fangs of the creature by waking in terror, he once more fell asleep." As he reenters the nightmare world, Clyde finds himself in a "strange and gloomy place, a wood or cave or narrow canyon," which uncovers "a score of reptiles, forked tongues and agate eyes" and "a horned and savage animal"—much like the dream of snakes and "monstrous animals with horns" of Poe's "The Thousand-and-Second Tale of Scheherazade." Clyde awakens from his dream, but its images thereafter color his vision of the landscape around Big Bittern.

The verbal patterns Dreiser employs to render the gothic quality of Clyde's perception of the lake district so nearly follow Poe's imagery as to rule out the possibility of mere coincidence. This does not mean, of course, that Dreiser necessarily had Poe opened at his side as he wrote these chapters. Anyone familiar with Dreiser's use of other sources in his writing knows that he did one of two things in such cases. He often made notes of his reading to which he later turned or, as is most likely in this case, he recalled verbal patterns he had absorbed years before. His memory was prodigious in this respect; for instance, he could dictate new drafts of his work from memory years after earlier drafts with an almost verbatim duplication of the earlier texts.

The shape the Big Bittern region takes in Clyde's mind when he first identifies the area as a possible site for Roberta's "accident" illustrates the intense impression Poe's gothic imagery made on Dreiser's imagination. Clyde dwells on the "desolate and for the most part lonely character of the region . . . the decadent and weird nature of some of the bogs and tarns . . . which . . . were festooned with funereal or viperous vines . . . the soggy and decayed piles of fallen and criss-crossed logs . . . the green slime . . . the vine or moss-covered stumps and rotting logs . . . the muck and the poisonous grasses and water plants . . . in this almost tenantless region." He "carried away the impression that for solitude and charm — or at least mystery — this region could scarcely be matched."

On the second and final trip to Big Bittern, Clyde observes from his train seat pastoral scenes where he and Roberta spent happy hours; but his absorption in "the more inward scene which now so much more concerned him — the nature of the lake country around Big Bittern" negates the last moment of grace provided him. Upon his arrival, the lake appears to his mind's eye as an "especially arranged pool or tarn"; it is "black or dark like tar, and sentineled to the east and north by tall, dark pines — the serried spears of armed and watchful giants, as they now seemed to him — ogres almost." Here and there Clyde encounters a dead pine "ashen pale in the hard afternoon sun, its gaunt sapless arms almost menacingly outstretched." As he and Roberta step into the boat, the lake "seemed, not so much like water as oil — like molten glass." A bird's "sharp metallic cry" combines with the "Kit, kit, kit Ca-a-a-ah!" of the weir-weir bird to provide the only break in the unnatural silence before Roberta's death.

In these pages Dreiser evokes the dark, lifeless underside of nature that often lay unexpressed beneath more optimistic nineteenth-century romantic visions of nature. Nurtured as we are on twentieth-century wasteland imagery, we tend to forget that such imagery has roots in the nineteenth century. Charles L. Campbell, for instance, argues that Dreiser wrote his novel "in conscious relation to Thoreau's vision of life in the woods," that is, as a deliberate inversion of Thoreau's American pastoral landscape — a landscape that Campbell takes as the American literary norm. This interpretation fails to recognize that Poe, not Dreiser, first gave us what Campbell calls "the most explicit depiction of the corrupted Garden in American literature." Poe's landscapes contain "strange trees waving to and fro their skeleton arms" (*Pym*), "the giants of the forest" ("The Sphinx"), with their "ghastly tree stems"

("Usher"); the constant "terror of the lone lake" ("The Lake: To—"), "so mirror-like was the glassy water" ("The Island of Fay"), "crystal lakes and over-arching forests ("Politian"); there are the ominous "dismal tarns and pools" ("Dream-land"), the regions of "extensive decay" ("Usher"); and the ever-present birds whose "metallic" cries—like the "Tekeli-li" at the end of *Pym*—are staples of Poe's work.

If Poe's nightmare landscapes provided Dreiser with the images to describe Clyde's separation from the life of nature, his poetry offered additional metaphors for the dreamlike state that attends the individual's alienation from his fellow creatures. William Phillips's fine study of the imagery of Dreiser's novels contends that water and tales of magic supply the main source of imagery in *An American Tragedy*, and that " 'dream' [is] the key word of this novel." A similar conclusion might be applied to a study of Poe's poetry about dream flights from the material world.

> By the lakes that thus outspread
> Their lone waters, lone and dead,—
> Their sad waters, sad and chilly
> With the snows of the lolling lily—
> By the mountains—near the river
> Murmuring lowly, murmuring ever,—
> By the grey woods,—by the swamp
> Where the toad and the newt encamp,—
> By the dismal tarns and pools
> Where dwell the Ghouls,—
> By each spot the most unholy—
> In each nook most melancholy,—
> There the traveller meets, aghast,
> Sheeted Memories of the Past—
>
> ("Dream-land," ll. 21–34)

In Poe, one travels through dream-land at his own risk; for the dream process includes the dissolution of material reality and of finite life—the very danger to which Clyde (and Roberta) fall victim on the lake. The dreamer often succumbs to a lotus-land, a form of spiritual death.

> For the heart whose woes are legion
> 'Tis a peaceful, soothing region
> For the spirit that walks in shadow
> 'Tis—Oh, 'tis an Eldorado

> But the traveller, travelling through it,
> May not—dare not openly view it.
>
> ("Dream-land," ll. 39–44)

So Clyde on the lake wanders hypnotically into a realm of ultimate illusion: "this pool or tarn was encircled by trees! And cat-tails and water lilies here and there—a few along the shores. And somehow suggesting an especially arranged pool or tarn to which one who was weary of life and cares—anxious to be away from the strife and contentions of the world, might most wisely and gloomily repair." Clyde dares to peer into the lake at this moment, and he finds that the peace it offers is the peace of "Death! Death! More definitely than anything he had ever seen before. Death! But also a still, quiet, unprotesting type of death into which one, by reason of choice or hypnosis or unutterable weariness, might joyfully and gratefully sink. So quiet—so shaded—so serene." Shortly after, Clyde looks into the water a second time. Now it no longer mirrors a dream of his own death; it reflects the vision, as from a crystal ball, of Roberta "struggling and waving her thin white arms out of the water and reaching toward him." As in poems like "Dream-land" and "Ulalume," the lake presents the traveler two images of death— the one a final dreamlike haven, the other a chilling vision of a dead lover's face.

In both instances Clyde can no longer see his own reflection in the lake. This condition bespeaks the form of spiritual death that in Poe is signaled by increasing abstraction from physical reality and withdrawal into private dream reveries. The words of "Berenice's" narrator, who inhabits too long "the very regions of fairy land"—a key term in Dreiser's novel—, could serve as a commentary on Clyde's predicament: "The realities of the world affected me as visions, and as visions only, while the wild ideas of the land of dreams became, in turn, not the material of my every-day existence, but in very deed that existence utterly and solely in itself." Poe conceived this state of mind as the precondition for the most terrifying plunges into insanity, often resulting in homicidal acts.

From the moment Clyde first contemplates murder, he becomes the victim of his own thoughts. As the idea of murder increasingly possesses him, the human reality of Roberta fades. By the time Clyde steps into the boat on Big Bittern, Roberta has lost human identity and the lake has become a dream: "an almost nebulous figure, she now seemed, stepping down into an insubstantial rowboat upon a purely ideational lake." Like a Berenice or a Lady Rowena, Roberta becomes an idea in a lifeless landscape: "To be sure, there was Roberta over there, but by now she had faded to a shadow or thought really, a form of illusion more vaporous than real. And while there was something about her in color, form that suggested reality—still she was very insubstantial—so very—and once more now he felt strangely alone." Roberta becomes real again for Clyde only after she sinks to the bottom of Big Bittern. Like the narrator of "Berenice"—who is startled into reality by "the shrill and piercing shriek of a female voice [that] seemed to be ringing in my ears. I had done a deed—what was it?"—Clyde awakens to a horror, bewildered and questioning his role in the deed: "Had he? Or, had he not?" The answer, as Dreiser intended, is complex. It is made even more so by the compelling influence of two forces in Clyde's psychic landscape—an evil genie and a solitary bird. With these creatures Dreiser achieved his most audacious and imaginative transformation of Poe.

II

It is a commonplace that *The Arabian Nights* provided Dreiser with a source of imagery to describe Clyde's fantasy life. Early in the novel Clyde perceives the cheap gaudiness of the Green-Davidson hotel as "a realization of paradise"; the new-found fortune in tips, "dimes, nickels, quarters and half dollars even," appears to him as "fantastic, Aladdinish, really." If Dreiser made no further use of *The Arabian Nights*, we would be inclined to write it off as at best a more sophisticated version of the oriental clichés that populated nineteenth-century romances—and Dreiser's novels from *Sister Carrie* on. But in chapter 45 Dreiser took a daring and richly melodramatic step by evoking the evil genie of the fisherman's tale to represent Clyde's darker subconscious desires.

> Indeed, it was now as though from the depths of some lower or higher world never before guessed or plumbed by him . . . there had now suddenly appeared, as the genii at the accidental rubbing of Aladdin's lamp—as the efrit emerging as smoke from the mystic jar in the net of the fisherman—the very substance of some leering and diabolical wish or wisdom concealed in his own nature.

The efrit takes total hold of Clyde, limiting his ability to act freely.

> Indeed the center or mentating section of his brain at this time might well have been compared to a sealed and silent hall in which alone and undisturbed, and that in spite of himself, he now sat thinking on the mystic or evil and terrifying desires or advice of some darker or primordial and unregenerate nature of his own,

and without the power to drive the same forth or himself to decamp.

From this point to Roberta's death, the efrit controls the "mentating section of [Clyde's] brain" with the power of a genie of old: "Behold! I bring you a way. It is the way of the lake." Dreiser shows us Clyde debating with the evil spirit, but the latter's logic prevails:

The Way of the Lake
The Way of the Lake

As I have mentioned, the inner cast given to *The Arabian Nights* imagery and the increased reliance on dream language has been taken as the offspring of Dreiser's steady interest in Freud in the years preceding *An American Tragedy*. The Freudian language and concepts of the novel suggest that Dreiser undoubtedly found reinforcement in Freud and A. A. Brill for his use of the efrit as an embodiment of Clyde's destructive unconscious impulses. However, Dreiser's more immediate sources are Poe's *Arabian Nights* tales, with their numerous "evil genii" and oriental demons that possess souls. In particular, Dreiser made extensive use of the murderous narrator's story in "The Imp of the Perverse."

The "Imp's" narrator begins with a lengthy discourse on the mystery of "perverseness," a term that corresponds in Poe to a blend of what Freud would later call masochism and the death-wish. "It is a radical, a primitive impulse . . . [which] under certain conditions . . . is often the one unconquerable *force* which impels us . . . to do wrong for the wrong's sake." To illustrate the mechanics of such irrational behavior, Poe turns to a familiar source:

> [When confronted with a repulsive temptation] our first impulse is to shrink from the danger. Unaccountably we remain. By slow degrees our sickness, and dizziness and horror, become merged in a cloud of unnameable feeling. By gradations, still more imperceptible, this cloud assumes shape, as did the vapor from the bottle out of which arose the genius in the Arabian Nights. But out of this *our* cloud upon the precipice's edge, there grows into palpability a shape, far more terrible than any genius, or any demon of a tale, and yet it is but a thought, although a fearful one, and one which chills the very marrow of our bones with the fierceness of the delight of its horror . . . [which] involves that one most ghastly and loathsome of all the most ghastly and loathsome images of death and suffering which have ever presented themselves to

our imagination. . . . There is no power in nature so demonically impatient. . . . To indulge for a moment, in any attempt at a *thought,* is to be inevitably lost, for reflection but urges us to forbear, and *therefore* it is, I say, that we *cannot.* If there be no friendly arm to check us . . . we plunge and are destroyed.

Dreiser found in this passage a narrative device to dramatize the demonic possession that leads to Clyde's fatal commitment to the way of the lake. The point, of course, is that Dreiser's use of the efrit had more to do with his reading of Poe than with Freud or Brill, and thus Clyde's psychology in these chapters derives mainly from literary not clinical sources. Following Poe's example, Dreiser represents the force that deadens the conscious will as a powerful evil genie. However, Dreiser transforms the slim possibility of salvation through the intercession of a "friendly arm" into the genie's "friendly sympathetic hands laid firmly on [Clyde's] shoulders. The comfort of them! The warmth! . . . the hands of this friend!" — thus emphasizing the severely determined course of Clyde's fate as, in Poe's phrase, "one of the many uncounted victims of the Imp of the Perverse."

Poe's victim, like Dreiser's, conceives his murder plan through the medium of the printed word — in Poe's case a French memoir that recounts a death "through the agent of a candle accidently poisoned. The idea struck my fancy at once." Unlike Clyde, however, he succeeds, and inherits the estate of his victim. Nor does the genie in Poe's tale provide the impulse to murder; the narrator, both more cold-blooded and self-sufficient than Clyde, can kill without aid from his "darker or primordial" self. The "perverseness" that fascinates Poe is the urge to confess that overtakes the murderer. "I became blind, and deaf, and giddy; and then, some invisible fiend, I thought, struck me with his broad palm upon the back. The long-imprisoned secret burst forth from my soul." Dreiser reworks the role of the evil genie to meet the demands of Clyde's character; he removes the demonic, unconscious urge from the murderer's psychopathic act of revelation and relocates it in the more sinister drive that incites Clyde to murder. Dreiser views the efrit as a force at once in Clyde and yet separate from his powers of volition, a supernatural figure that makes plausible a "moral coward's" capacity to plan murder. Dreiser's more complex characterization focuses on this force in Clyde's psyche to dramatize the ambiguous nature of guilt. Clyde's "perverseness," though couched in the exotic framework invented by Poe, thus leads us to consider a more central aspect of crime and punishment.

It might be well to recall here that the use of the Poe-like efrit as a supernatural agent came readily to Dreiser's mind. His interest in the supernatural, after all, did not begin with Poe. The opening chapter of his autobiography *Dawn* is set in an aura of magic—in the form of three spirits that visited his mother at the time of his birth. During Dreiser's newspaper days in the 1890s, he reported on theosophy, telepathy, and mediums; he had the habit of consulting fortune tellers; he joined seances during World War I; he was enormously attracted to Charles Fort; he wrote plays of the supernatural, employed the Macbeth witches in the Cowperwood novels, and by the 1930s wrote of electricity as a kind of oversoul. Poe, then, offered Dreiser a literary precedent—and a literary idiom—for a concern that was life-long.

III

Along with the efrit, an equally mysterious creature follows Clyde as he rows Roberta to her death by water. Clyde encountered this other being during his first trip to Big Bittern. At that time Clyde found himself mulling over the incident at Pass Lake: In the process "his own subconscious need was contemplating the loneliness and the usefulness at times of such a lone spot as this. And at one point it was that a wier-wier, one of the solitary water-birds of this region, uttered its ouphe and barghest cry." Clyde "stirred nervously. . . . It was so very different to any bird-cry he had ever heard before." When he questions a companion about the strange sound, the following interchange occurs.

> "What?"
> "Why, that bird or something that just flew away back there just now?"
> "I didn't hear any bird."
> "Gee! That was a queer sound. It makes me feel creepy."

In this way Dreiser introduces—tongue in cheek, I am tempted to say—"one of the solitary water-birds of the region" who is audible always only to Clyde.

Ever since John T. Flanagan verified the weir-weir as "a bird apparently as unknown to ornithology as the roc or the phoenix," readers have tried to account for its origin. Most logically attribute the name to a play upon "the common use of 'weird' as a synonym for 'strange.'" Richard Lehan correctly assumes that the bird has its roots in romantic symbolism and that Dreiser adds a "gothic quality to the symbol, making the bird reflect a demonic element." Lehan proposes that weir is a "pun on the Anglo-Saxon word 'wyrd'—that is, fate." However, one need not go so far afield to find the origin of the weir-weir.

> Then my heart it grew ashen and sober
> As the leaves that were crisped and sere—
> As the leaves that were withering and sere;
> And I cried: "It was surely October
> On *this* very night of last year
> That I journeyed—I journeyed down here!—
> That I brought a dead burden down here—
> On this night of all nights of the year,
> Ah, what demon has tempted me here?
> Well, I know, now, this dim lake of Auber—
> This misty mid region of Weir—
> Well, I know, now, this dank tarn of Auber
> This ghoul-haunted woodland of Weir.
>
> ("Ulalume," ll. 82–94)

Dreiser identified the bird twice in the novel, first as the "wier-wier" and the second time—when Roberta is drowning—as the "weir-weir." (He originally named it once again, calling it the "weir-weir," in the last paragraph of book 2 but changed it in the galleys to "that bird.") The reason for this discrepancy is to be found in the manuscripts and typescripts of the novel housed in the special collection at the University of Pennsylvania. The original handwritten manuscript reveals that Dreiser wrote the bird's name as "wier-weir" in the first passage, the Dreiser-like metathesis occurring only in the first half of the name. The first typed copy shows that the typist simply copied the first spelling twice, a spelling that went unaltered through two additional revised typescripts, two sets of galleys, the first edition and each edition since. Neither editor nor critic seems to have noticed the difference between the first and second naming of the bird—though in critical commentaries it is always referred to correctly as the "weir-weir." In any case, in its capacity as the ruling spirit of the region, the weir-weir serves as an emblem of—and a cryptic tribute to—the guiding spirit behind Dreiser's imagination in these chapters.

Scholars are not certain of Poe's source for "Weir," but Dreiser was less concerned with Poe's source than with "Ulalume's" thematic relevance to his novel. It is one of Poe's most sophisticated poems about the lure of true and false ideals of beauty. The themes of poems like "Ulalume," "To One in Paradise," and "The Lake: To—" explain Dreiser's reliance on their imagery as he plotted out his woodland murder. The poems work on a more abstract plane than the novel, but the basic theme of conflict between ideal and mundane loves is common to both. Dreiser gave an ironic twist to Poe's quest for ideal beauty by locating "beauty" for a Clyde in the meretricious artifacts and fetishes of middle-American culture. In this context, Sondra's world offers Clyde the promise of an earthly paradise; Roberta's offers the mundane reality of a life whose limits Clyde knows too well. If Dreiser discovered analogues to his theme in Poe's writing, he also found Poe's language and imagery appropriate to his story of a young man's tragic dreams of wealth and poverty. Clyde succumbs to his dreams in a region reminiscent of Weir. Yet, unlike the lover in "Ulalume," he is unable either to redeem himself from the spell cast by his false ideal, Sondra, or to reunite with the lost Roberta. Clyde can only follow the promptings of the evil genie and "the voice of that weird, contemptuous mocking, lonely bird."

Though "Ulalume" supplied Dreiser with the strange bird's name, "The Raven" had still more to do with the language and symbolism surrounding the weir-weir's deadly interchange with Clyde. In "The Philosophy of a Composition," Poe identified his "bird of ill omen" as a messenger of "Death — . . . the death, then, of a beautiful woman [which] is unquestionably, the most poetical topic in the world." The Raven, "emblematical of Mournful and Never-ending Remembrance," repeats variations of the refrain " 'Nevermore' to the lover's final demand if he shall meet his mistress in another world." Poe said that the poem's composition began, significantly, with the stanza reflecting the speaker's most intense anxiety.

> "Prophet," said I, "thing of evil! prophet still if bird or devil!
> By what heaven that bends above us — by that God we both adore
> Tell this soul with sorrow laden, if within the distant Aidenn,
> It shall clasp a sainted maiden whom the angels name Lenore —
> Clasp a rare and radiant maiden whom the angels name Lenore."
> Quoth the raven "Nevermore."

Given the terms of the poem, we might expect Dreiser to employ his bird to foreshadow Clyde's loss of Sondra. (In fact, he does echo the poem earlier in the novel, as when we learn that Clyde "dreamed into [Sondra's] eyes as might a devotee into those of a saint". But Sondra is no true Lenore to Clyde, and so Dreiser's bird is put to more ominous use, The weir-weir does not speak in human tones but its refrain proves as insistent as the raven's.

> Kit, kit, kit, Ca-a-a-ah!
> Kit, kit, kit, Ca-a-a-ah!
> Kit, kit, kit, Ca-a-a-ah!

With this cry, the bird heralds Roberta's death and intensifies Clyde's anxiety. In language strikingly similar to that of "The Raven," Clyde listens to "the cry of the devilish bird upon that dead limb." The "unearthly bird" stations itself as fixedly on the limb of the dead tree as Poe's raven upon the bust of Pallas. Clyde's internal address to the bird restates the question posed by Poe's speaker: "What was it [the bird] sounding—a warning—a protest—condemnation? The same bird that had marked the very birth of this miserable plan. For there it was now upon that dead tree—that wretched bird." The bird remains silently upon the limb, until Roberta falls into the lake. As she drowns, Clyde hears once more its refrain mingling with the voice of the efrit: "The cry of that devilish bird upon that dead limb—the weir-weir."

The degree to which Dreiser was absorbed by the rhythms of "The Raven" as he wrote these pages can be gauged by the extension of the poem's language beyond the weir-weir's immediate compass. For example, the raven's persistent "tapping, tapping at my chamber door" can be heard in "the lone and ghostly tap-tap-tap of some solitary woodpecker." More importantly, variations of the bird's refrain—"Nameless *here* for evermore"; "Never—nevermore"—become part of Clyde's own refrain. Under the pressure of the weir-weir's "weird, haunting cry," Clyde reflects that "They would not come on shore again together. Never! Never!" When the boat capsizes it is the "Efrit of his own darker self" that tempts Clyde to ignore Roberta's pleas for help: "Behold. It is over. She is sinking now. You will never, never see her alive any more—ever."

The irony implicit in Clyde's internalization of "The Raven's" message stems from Dreiser's more somber version of his source. The poem's speaker laments his "lost Lenore"; Clyde's refrain is no lament but an ominous accompaniment to Roberta's end. It subsequently proves to be "emblematical of Mournful and Neverending Remembrance"—of murder. Clyde would be pursued by the memory of Roberta's last moments; she, not a weird bird, haunts the chambers of his mind: "Ghosts! Hers . . . ghosts—God—spirits that might pursue you after they were dead, seeking to expose and punish you—seeking to set people on your track, maybe! Who could tell? His mother . . . believed in ghosts." Clyde remains, to the end, like Roderick Usher, "a victim to the terrors he had anticipated."

Dreiser's reshaping of Poe's imagery and themes went into the making of one of the finest narrative sequences in modern American fiction. This fact alone should prompt us to rethink those easy literary assumptions that place artificial walls between our so-called romantic and realistic writers. In dealing with any important writer, the challenge that confronts a critic is to explain how the artist turns what he does into *poetry*. In Dreiser's case, despite all the abuse heaped upon his style, the *best* of his prose is more a form of poetry—in the high romantic (1790–1840) mode—than most eulogized fiction since 1890. Dreiser's use of Poe is only one example of how he transmutes his romantic sources into a modern kind of poetry that is at once tender, deeply reflective of conflict, specifically local in flavor, and universal in its breadth of application. Dreiser's subtle reworking of Poe also argues against the idea of Dreiser as a "primitive," an instinctual writer who has no literary or intellectual roots and who achieved powerful effects as a plodding recorder of "real" experience. On the contrary, *An American Tragedy* is evidence of a remarkable "collaboration"—a testament to the staying power of ideas and language, and to the bonds that unite creative effort across the generations.

Technique as Theme
in *An American Tragedy*

Paul A. Orlov

It was a critical commonplace, until recently, that Theodore Dreiser is a writer who cannot write, whose novels, whatever their merits, manifest little technical prowess. According to this timeworn myth—perhaps perpetuated even today in some critical quarters and classrooms—Dreiser's fiction reads (to paraphrase an old adage) as if it had been produced by an infinite number of monkeys pounding away at an infinite number of typewriters. Even the novelist's supporters and admirers typically made modest claims for his artistry, or conceded its deficiencies. An early, extreme example of such response appears in H. L. Mencken's review of *An American Tragedy:* while praising the book as "a human document . . . searching and full of a solemn dignity" that sometimes "rises to the level of genuine tragedy," Mencken denounces it artistically as "a colossal botch" and finds it "shapeless."

Granting that Mencken's view is characteristically more exaggerated and less reliable than the evaluations of some objective critics one might cite, we must nonetheless note that he shows an interesting imperceptiveness seen traditionally in *many* critics' comments on Dreiser: he oddly overlooks the problems posed by claiming a poorly crafted work has a powerful impact. A recent objection to such reasoning has been offered by Robert Penn Warren, whose own achievements as a writer and critic make his remarks particularly persuasive. With reference to those qualities almost all commentators have paid tribute to in *An American Tragedy* and its author's other best fiction, Warren asks:

From *The Journal of Narrative Technique* 14, no. 2 (Spring 1984). © 1984 by *The Journal of Narrative Technique.*

> But ultimately how do we know the "power" or "compassion"
> . . . except by Dreiser's control? Except, in other words, by the
> rhythmic organization of his materials, the vibrance which is the
> life of fictional illusion, the tension among elements, and the mutual
> interpenetration in meaning of part and whole which gives us the
> sense of preternatural fulfillment? Except, in short, by art?

For all its general appraisal as a masterpiece, *An American Tragedy* has not yet received sufficient study in technical terms to disclose dimensions of Dreiser's fictional art that are central to the novel's purport and power. Despite several critics' important insights into the book's technical elements, I believe some of the most essential ways in which Dreiser creates (in Warren's words) "tension among elements, and the mutual interpenetration in meaning of part and whole," have not been noted. Specifically, there has not been adequate recognition of the complex correspondence that exists between narrative technique and theme in *An American Tragedy*.

While many discussions of the novel have mentioned Clyde Griffiths's role-playing in relation to the fundamental theme of his tragic quest after the American "dream of success," a few interpretations have indicated, in their own ways, the deepest ramifications of roles he compulsively adopts in the pursuit: the doomed pursuit involves damaging distortions of Clyde's individual identity itself. In fact, as I have elsewhere documented in detail, there is considerable evidence in the text that the theme of the self is crucial to the novel's design: Dreiser dramatizes the ways in which identity is imperilled by blind belief in the materialistic values and illusory opportunities of the Success-ideal; *An American Tragedy* is about the figurative destruction of Clyde's selfhood by false values, as well as about his literal destruction by the Alger myth enshrining those values. And my purpose here, after briefly explaining the essential theme of selfhood in the novel, will be to show how Dreiser uses several complementary narrative methods that help both express and extend that thematic emphasis.

I

When the young Clyde receives his initial exposure to that worldly life from which his poor, missionary parents hold themselves totally apart, his response reveals not only his character, but also an attitude curiously crucial to true understanding of the novel. Working for a soda fountain adjacent to a popular theatre, Clyde excitedly observes well-dressed boys enjoying various pleasures with pretty girls. From these observations spring his incipient sense that money and fine clothes are required for sexual fulfillment and all of life's fun, and his resultant determination to pursue purposes utterly unlike his parents':

> No good-looking girl, as it then appeared to him, would have any-thing to do with him if he did not possess this [sartorial] standard of equipment. It was plainly necessary—the thing. And once he did attain it—was able to wear such clothes as these—well, then was he not well set upon the path that leads to all the blisses?

> You bet he would get out of [the self-denying, materially impoverished realm of religious "rewards"] now. He would work and save his money and be somebody.

The importance of the last sentence of this passage—of its final two words in particular—cannot be too strongly stressed. Far from being merely a casual "figure of speech," Clyde's idea that an acquisition of wealth will allow him to "be somebody" metaphorically suggests the belief (absorbed from his society) that personal significance and dignity are purchasable, but by no means inherent. And the assumptions involved in this belief—that appearances and essences are the same, that what one *has* determines "who" he *is*, and that "success" can therefore forge an identity—are implicitly criticized by Dreiser's 1925 masterpiece as a source of direly destructive effects on both human relationships and individual lives like Clyde Griffiths's.

Ironically, both the naturalistic quality of his fiction and the pro-nouncements in his polemical writings have sometimes led to the mistaken view that Theodore Dreiser does not believe in, let alone affirm the intrinsic value of, each person's essential identity or selfhood. It is true that the deterministic elements in Dreiser's novels tend to emphasize the expression of impersonal forces, rather than personalities principally expressed through will; it is also true that in various nonfictional works, such as an essay bluntly titled "The Myth of Individuality," Dreiser denies the essential uniqueness of each person's identity, contending that human nature and behavior involve few fundamental variations and are ultimately explainable by "laws" of mechanistic science (including physiological psychology). But enlightened criticism has long recognized, nonetheless, that in his fiction, Dreiser is at least a very "inconsistent mechanist." Applying this phrase to the novelist in his seminal study, Eliseo Vivas observes how little likeness Dreiser's artistic vision of life bears to the coldly objective theories of mechanism. For indeed, how could Dreiser have written novels whose impact on generations of readers has often been related to his celebratedly compassionate characterizations, without an intense humanistic engagement in the reality and meaning of individual lives? Further, the work of Malcolm Cowley and, more recently, Donald Pizer has helped to correct simplistic suppositions about the treatment of "individuality" in the context of literary naturalism. A statement by Pizer redefining "naturalism" in general has particular pertinence to the case of Dreiser in the depiction of Clyde Griffiths:

> The naturalist often describes his characters as though they are conditioned and controlled by environment, heredity, instinct, or chance. But he also suggests a compensating humanistic value in his characters or their fates which affirms the significance of the individual and his life. . . . The naturalist appears to say that although the individual may be a cipher in a world made amoral by man's lack of responsibility for his fate, the imagination refuses to accept this formula as the total meaning of life and so seeks a new basis for man's sense of his own dignity and importance. The naturalistic novel is therefore not so superficial or reductive as it implicitly appears to be in its conventional definition.

Clearly, a novel's intentions are not simply the same as those its author objectively maintains; artistic imagination, rather than conscious theory, serves as the dominant shaping force in fiction. And we can therefore discover that in *An American Tragedy*, Dreiser, far from denying his characters' intrinsic individuality and importance, in fact illuminates a materialistic society's indifference to the dignity of the self as a root cause of the tragedy in their midst—that tragedy embodied in the life and death of Clyde Griffiths.

That the novel *does* represent an implicit defense of the self against the dehumanizing obsession with appearances and possessions of a Success-driven society, can be readily revealed by underscoring a few key passages in, and major aspects of, its plot. Dreiser's use of language and plot motifs repeatedly reinforces the idea in the soda fountain scene that for Clyde, being "somebody" means having money and looking "successful." After his brief soda fountain novitiate, Clyde becomes fully initiated into the religion of worldly values and ways of seeing in the gaudily materialistic Green-Davidson Hotel. There he observes the pleasures and privileges of the wealthy, the "correct" fashions and manners, and, most crucially, the socio-economic significance of identities: "This, then, most certainly was what it meant *to be rich, to be a person of consequence* in the world—to have money. It meant that you did what you pleased. That other people, like himself, waited upon you. That you possessed all of these luxuries. That you went how, where and when you pleased" (emphasis mine). Convinced conclusively that only money confers importance and power upon a person in his society, Clyde starts playing roles calculated to make him look like, or be liked by, those who (being successful) *matter*. In this process, he learns how to dress, speak, act, and think in order to attract an employer, a good tip, a friend, or a pretty girl. Thus Clyde's initial quest for individual status involves him, through denial of his family origins and distortion of his nature for social acceptance, in a gradual obscuring of his actual identity.

Later, after capitalizing on the proper persona to get a job in Chicago's Union League Club and to impress there his fortuitously met rich uncle, Clyde moves to Lycurgus for the major phase of his misguided pursuit of that individual *worth* too literally defined by society. In book 2 of the novel, depicting Clyde's rise and fall in the small city dominated by his rich relatives, Dreiser's techniques repeatedly reveal the thematic emphasis on the Success-ethic's subversion of true selfhood. Just after his arrival, Clyde searches through the splendor of Wykeagy Avenue wealth until he finds the Samuel Griffiths mansion. Words aptly convey worldview in his reflections while looking at the imposing residence:

> For consider *who the Griffiths were* here, as opposed to "who" the Griffiths were in Kansas City, say—or Denver. The enormous difference! . . . Oh, the devil—who was he anyway? And *what did he* really *amount to*? What could he hope for from such a great world as this really . . . ? A little disgusted and depressed, he turned to retrace his steps, for all at once *he felt himself* very much *a nobody*. (Emphases mine.)

Yet the ambitious youth's discouraged appraisal of himself and his chances for rags-to-riches advancement is short-lived, for it soon becomes obvious to him that mere relatedness to wealth makes him *seem* "someone" important in the Lycurgus world: being "a Griffiths" so enhances the status of "who" Clyde "is" in this new environment, that he quickly wins a marked deference from most others except his relatives and their fellow patricians. And the benefits of this deference—ranging from the courtesy of coworkers in the Griffiths factory, to the friendly respect of people in diverse everyday contexts, to the compliantly amorous warmth of women such as Roberta Alden—inflate Clyde's illusions about his identity and prospects in a peculiarly dangerous way.

Of course, Clyde Griffiths's tragically ironic career based on what might be called "gilt by association" also derives much of its impetus from his remarkable resemblance to his rich cousin Gilbert. Dreiser's use of this "double" motif, conspicuous contrivance though it may be, quite effectively emphasizes society's superficiality and expresses the implicit theme of imperilled identity.

Living in a world obsessed with externals and looking strikingly like a wealthy youth whose prestigious name he shares, Clyde, in many eyes, virtually seems synonymous with that double. Seeming to be Gilbert's alter ego first earns Clyde his uncle's attention and invitation to Lycurgus "opportunity"; in time, it gains him promotion from menial labor to a position of pseudoauthority in the family factory, since Samuel, shocked at the sight of his son's likeness in sweat-stained garb, wants his nephew to "wear a decent suit of clothes and *look like*" (though he is condescendingly considered not to *be*) "somebody" (emphasis mine). The community's "common" folk see Clyde as an uncommon individual of great present or potential stature precisely because they mistake his famous face and name as the *essence of* his identity. Thus, Roberta Alden, herself eager to touch a materialized dream of success, thrills at the interest of Clyde, compromises her morals to keep him, and thinks him worth wedding despite months of mistreatment at his hands, principally because of "who" Clyde's distinguished double suggests he *is* or soon will be. And even the embodiment of wealth and beauty for whom he abandons and plans to drown Roberta is drawn to Clyde by his familial features: Sondra Finchley, intrigued by his resemblance to Gilbert (enhanced by social skills Clyde carefully acquires or counterfeits), becomes the genie apparently promising to fulfill all of Clyde's ambitious dreams. With these strong encouragements of his belief in becoming another Gilbert Griffiths, that visible incarnation of his fantasy-self of wealth and power, Clyde quite misjudges others' personal "worth," as well as his own potentiality, by exclusively extrinsic criteria: Roberta seems unworthy of him, "[f]or after all, who was she? A factory girl! The daughter of parents who lived and worked on a farm and one who was compelled to work for her own living. Whereas he—he—if fortune would but favor him a little!" And when "fortune" does "favor him" in the person of the sacredly idealized Sondra, just when the poor "factory girl" becomes pregnant and threatening, there appears to his materialistic mind a compellingly complete contrast: "The difference between . . . these girls—Sondra with everything offering all—asking nothing of him; Roberta, with nothing, asking all." Moved by such assumptions, and unable to escape the consequences of his double-life because, ironically, he lacks his "double's" power (mental or financial) to deal with the problem of unwanted pregnancy, Clyde is led inexorably toward the nightmarish ending of his Success-dreams, on Big Bittern Lake.

What follows Clyde's arrest after the death of Roberta is not merely the punishment of a crime of ambition which society itself, as Dreiser explains in a key essay related to the novel, has helped make too likely; for this punishment in turn betokens a betrayal by society, in a tragically ironic manner, of its Algeresque promise that success-seeking, even at the cost of self-betrayal, can culminate in true self-actualization. Having overreached himself in a self-destructive attempt at self-creation encouraged by others' indifference to his intrinsic identity, Clyde is then judged and condemned without ever being *understood* in purely *personal* terms. Lonely in the ultimate degree throughout his misguided search for meaningful selfhood, he is put to death by a society indifferent (in both its values and its verdict) to the realities of his individual life.

II

Narrative technique crucially complements thematic thrust in *An American Tragedy*. Dreiser's tacit defense of the self against the destructive force of materialistic values in a modern mass society finds both expression and emphasis through his adept use of three devices essential to the novel's narrative design: structural parallels between the three "books" of the novel pointedly punctuate the protagonist's plight; shifts in the narrator's "voice" obliquely offset a view prevailing in the world depicted; and the last section of the story (book 3) serves as an ironic commentary on the tragic significance of the whole work. Each of these devices contributes to the total impact that the novel achieves because of its interpenetration of method and meaning.

Parallel structures connecting the three major stages of Clyde's story to each other and to the theme of imperilled identity have an important effect in the developing dramatization of his "American tragedy." While some of these structures have been observed by many readers, neither the extent nor the significance of the ways in which plot parallels weave the work together has been sufficiently noticed. The opening scene of the novel immediately implies the thematic emphasis on identity in the striking nature of its narration:

> Dusk—of a summer night.
>
> And the tall walls of the commercial heart of an American city of perhaps 400,000 inhabitants—such walls as in time may linger as a mere fable.
>
> And up the broad street, now comparatively hushed, a little band of six. . . .
>
> Crossing at right angles the great thoroughfare on which they walked, was a second canyon-like way, threaded by throngs and vehicles and various lines of cars which clanged their bells and made such progress as they might amid swiftly moving streams of traffic. Yet the little group seemed unconscious of anything save a set purpose to make its way between the contending lines of traffic and pedestrians which flowed by them.

The twilight atmosphere, and the contrast between the vast city and that slow-moving "little group" surrounded by its swift spectacle, emphasize the estrangement of individuals from their modern mass society. And the several pages following these initial paragraphs in turn sugest the separateness of a boy of twelve from the rest of his "unimportant-looking family publicly raising its collective voice against the vast skepticism and apathy of" commerical urban "life." For all the differences in historical moment and subject matter, the narrative technique in these opening pages is rather like that used by Cooper at the start of *The Prairie* (1827): indistinct figures emerge into the foreground against a backdrop of overpowering presence, suggesting the impersonality and utter indifference to individuals of that environment (the "canyon-like" walls of a modern city now instead of the barren, uncivilized plains) within which the figures must make their way. At the same time, the indefiniteness of the boy of twelve's identity is made clear by the fact that in his alienation from his family's religious life and his exclusion from the very different life he wonderingly watches in the streets, he is not even named until the first chapter's last paragraphs.

The focus of the narration then narrows to Clyde as he begins pursuing an identity in that high-walled coldly commercial city symbolizing the material pleasures and beauties of his dawning desires. In this focal movement from the impersonal world to the individual seeking meaning within it, we find an anticipation of a tension between theme and technique vital to the whole book. Once we see, as both Robert Penn Warren and Donald Pizer have helpfully observed, that Dreiser's writing of the novel shows the influence of interest in cinematic effects and that the narrative sometimes seems based on a "fictional approximation of camera techniques," we have a figure for interpreting the thematic significance of shifts in focus. The openings of the novel's three "books" offer parallel perspectives on the world which shapes Clyde's life, as seen by the camera "eye" from a great distance; each book ends, conversely, with close-ups of Clyde, starkly exposing his experience as an individual in that social world. And the basic nature of that experience, his victimization in pursuing personal status, can be delineated in this meaningful matrix of parallel and contrasting camera views.

For in his use of this shifting perspective on the unfolding story, Dreiser develops a dialectic in structure expressive of the overall pattern of Clyde's tragic quest for selfhood. Dreiser makes it clear, implicitly in the novel and explicitly in a subsequent essay on the "American tragedy" pattern, that Clyde Griffiths (like his real-life counterparts) is condemned for failing to achieve the very goals the condemning society has set for him: ironically, only the criminal means he uses to achieve the ends to which a materialistic world urges him—uses only because illusory opportunities for success are blocked by social realities and personal limitations—put the aspirant in the role of reprobate outcast rather than heroic exemplar of the social ideal. This grim irony of Clyde's career in society is punctuated by the parallels that symbolize his destruction. Each book opens with an overview of the realm from which he seeks recognition as a meaningful person—the commercial city representing the values of the "American dream," in book 1; the specific sphere of his desperate reach toward that dream (in Lycurgus, ruled by his relatives' name), in book 2; and in book 3, the rural and small-town communities that overtly embody a moralistic self-righteousness punishing failure to attain pleasures and powers (of transgression) it covertly envies. Each book closes with an image of Clyde, a man "outside" in utter aloneness, in moments of deepening defeat: books 1 and 2, of course, end with strikingly similar scenes of his flight after ambiguous accidents—the car crash in Kansas City shattering his hotel life and hopes of enjoying Hortense, followed, more menacingly, by the drowning, soon ruinous to all his dreams—that leads to his labelling as a murderer and, in book 3's ending, his execution. Thus each configuration of contrasting scenes (at the start and close of a book) adumbrates Clyde's encounter with an environment remote in its indifference, accentuates the final futility and isolation of his state, and anticipates the descent toward doom of his quest to create a socially substantial self.

Just as shifts in the camera-eye's view of key scenes help to underline the basic nature of Clyde's plight in pursuing personhood, so do modulations in the narrator's voice obliquely help to undermine the false faiths of a society insidiously inducing such a plight. A second strategy in the novel's narration that intertwines with theme, Dreiser's careful use of point-of-view covertly comments on the dehumanizing of the individual by an America seeing self-realization in superficial terms.

One of the watchwords of Dreiser criticism (amidst diverse differences in interpretation and evaluation of the novelist) had always been "compassion." Thus in a valuable account of ways in which the writer transformed and transcended the factual materials of murder cases in creating Clyde's story, Donald Pizer notes that Dreiser's shaping of sources into fictional art partly depended on the "necessary stimulus" of "a vital emotional identification with his protagonist." Indeed, my contention is that Dreiser's *own* capacity for sympathetic understanding of the yearning self that is Clyde—dramatized by meaningful manipulation of point-of-view—is set against the nature of the very social forces his novel scrutinizes and reveals, in all *their* judgmental indifference.

Dreiser exploits two different narrative perspectives on the action in *An*

American Tragedy, sometimes using an objective, omniscient viewpoint to cast an impersonal light on his protagonist's experiences, sometimes seeing as if with Clyde's eyes and mind, through the technique of indirect discourse. This technique is itself a variation of third-person point-of-view, but in a form that approximates the effect of first-person narrative, affording us what seems direct access to Clyde's thoughts and feelings. Along with the juxtaposition of the two narrative stances, the very tension between the narrator's actual distance from his character and apparent absorption in that character makes indirect discourse an emblem of empathy which expresses, by contrast, the dire disregard of the world confronting Clyde. This is especially true since Dreiser turns increasingly to the narrative stance suggesting sympathy with his protagonist as Clyde's difficulties deepen, in books 2 and 3. And the device of indirect discourse has an indispensable impact on our reactions, as readers, to the novel's tragic characterizations.

While indirect discourse contributes to characterization throughout the novel, it is often offset in book 1 by objective or even ironically critical comments from the narrator on the ambitious youth being introduced. Representative of the way Dreiser both reveals Clyde's inner view and regards him with implicit irony is the end of the passage in which the soda-fountain spectacle makes the poor boy yearn to "save his money and *be somebody*": "Decidedly this simple and yet idyllic compound of the commonplace had all the luster and wonder of a spiritual transfiguration, the true mirage of the lost and thirsting and seeking victim of the desert." Here the inflated diction simultaneously portrays and punctures the vision of Clyde's worldly religion. Yet a few passages are more pointedly critical, such as that in which Clyde enters the first key formative environment of the Green-Davidson Hotel, as the narrator intrudes upon description of his wonder with a detachment diminishing the illusion:

> Once through [the door], he beheld a lobby . . . more arresting, quite, than anything he had seen before. It was all so lavish. Under his feet was a checkered black-and-white marble floor. Above him a coppered and stained and gilded ceiling. And supporting this, a veritable forest of black marble columns as highly polished as the floor—glassy smooth. And between the columns which ranged away . . . were lamps, statuary, rugs, palms, chairs, divans, tête-à-têtes—a prodigal display. In short it was compact, of all that gauche luxury of appointment which, as someone once sarcastically remarked, was intended to supply "exclusiveness to the masses." Indeed, for an essential hotel in a great and successful American

commercial city, it was almost too luxurious. . . .
He gazed about in awe and amazement.

And while Clyde's character is sometimes exposed in language and syntax realistically representative of his thoughts (as when the hotel's hiring of him leads to his ecstatic resolve to "wait and see just how much he would make here in this perfectly marvelous-marvelous realm"), Dreiser often observes him from a distance demanded by book 1's design to establish the protagonist's personality and patterns of response. Thus at the close of the book, after the auto accident, we watch Clyde trying "to hide—to lose himself and so escape—if the fates were only kind—the misery and the punishment and the unending dissatisfaction" which the situation "represented to him."

But such mere suggestions of Clyde's feelings from an objective angle generally gives way to charged "direct" depiction of them in the increasing reliance on indirect discourse in the novel's second section. Dreiser makes extensive use of this narrative technique in book 2 for intertwined purposes necessary for accomplishment of the work's intended "tragic" effect: he dramatizes his own sympathetic involvement with Clyde and, quite as crucially, involves his readers emotionally with Clyde. In a novel about a young man's futile quest to gain individualized recognition from his world, it is imperative that *we* find his individuality moving and important. Serving this end, the expression of Clyde's experiences through indirect discourse makes his reality powerfully present to us, increasingly guiding our response to his story from detachment toward distress, or even "from contempt toward compassion." Particularly significant in terms of the theme of selfhood is a passage illuminating Clyde's ideas about his cousin-double Gilbert, whose attitude toward even his eminent father is startlingly self-assured:

> How wonderful it must be to be a son who, without having had to earn all this, could still be so much, take oneself so seriously, exercise so much command and authority. It might be, as it plainly was, that this youth was very superior and indifferent in tone toward him. But think of being such a youth, having so much power at one's command!

Here diction denotes preoccupation in a manner curiously complementary to the impact of point-of-view: a palpable proliferation of forms of the verb "to be" in this passage (seven in all) insists upon Clyde's indeterminate sense of self and dangerous desire to *become* a youth just like Gilbert. Our awareness of the ache for individual status conveyed by Clyde's thoughts is accentuated by those moments, mirroring vividly his inner state, when he "fe[els] himself very much of a nobody" after gazing at the "grandeur" of his uncle's mansion, or, later, cannot consider Roberta a prospective mate despite his enjoyment of sexual intimacy with her, because that same house is "a shrine to him, nearly—the symbol of that height to which by some turn of fate he might still hope to attain." When that "turn of fate" seems to occur in the dawning interest in him of Sondra Finchley, his thrilled thoughts exult in "That wonderful girl! That beauty! That world of health and social position she live[s] in!"—leading him to ponder a portentous question: "And what harm . . . was there in a poor youth like himself aspiring to such heights? Other youths as poor as himself had married girls as rich as Sondra." And once the "harm" that indeed follows from this aspiration begins to impend, as Clyde struggles to free himself from Roberta for a future at Sondra's side, Dreiser engages us emotionally in the climactic part of the plot by increasingly dramatizing rather than describing Clyde's experiences, and by making much use of rapidfire series of short or fragmented sentences that simulate a stream-of-consciousness disclosure of Clyde's mind in desperate moments. This striking style is especially evident in the narrative of the novel's climax on Big Bittern Lake:

> And Clyde, as instantly sensing the profoundness of his own failure, his own cowardice or inadequateness for such an occasion, as instantly yielding to a tide of submerged hate, not only for himself, but Roberta—her power—or that of life to restrain him in this way. And yet fearing to act in any way—being unwilling to—being willing only to say that never, never would he marry her—that never, even should she expose him, would he leave here with her to marry her—that he was in love with Sondra and would cling only to her—and yet not being able to say that even. But angry and confused and glowering. And then, as [Roberta] drew near him, seeking to take his hand in hers and the camera from him in order to put it in the boat, he flinging out at her, but not even then with any intention to do other than free himself of her—her touch—her pleading . . . her presence forever—God!

Because of the close-up camera and the impetus of indirect discourse in passages like this, we are intensely involved in Clyde's plight precisely when he is most painfully alone with it, in the culmination—and aftermath—of book 2.

Similarly, the author's truly personal concern for the experiences defining Clyde, conveyed tellingly through narrative technique, stands as symbolic criticism of the total *lack* of concern for Clyde's individuality in the world that urges and encourages him to contrive a pseudo-self for "Success." There is a revealing moment shortly before his trial when Clyde considers why he had kept all the letters (from his mother, from Roberta, from Sondra) that helped lead quickly to his arrest after the drowning: "If only he had destroyed them. Roberta's, his mother's, all! Why hadn't he? But not being able to answer why—just an insane desire to keep things maybe—anything that *related to him—a kindness*, a tenderness *toward him*" (emphases mine). As this inner confession suggests, Clyde's life fabricating a false identity leaves him a hollow man, hungering for true connection with others. Far from being "insane," his "desire" for "things" relating personally to him is an utterly natural reaction against an unnatural way of being that prevents him, like Yank in Eugene O'Neill's *The Hairy Ape* (1922), from feeling that he *belongs* to a community within which he has individual importance. And ironically, the process of Clyde's arrest, trial, and punishment for his "crime" against society (in the person of Roberta), which gains him the recognition of infamy *in* the community, makes his identity (as I shall further show) more misunderstood than ever *by* it. Thus at the novel's close, as Clyde awaits execution, our intimate contact with him through indirect discourse is poignantly played off against the ultimate solitude of his situation:

> His youth. Kansas City. Chicago. Lycurgus. Roberta and Sondra. How swiftly they and all that was connected with them passed in review. The few, brief, bright intense moments. His desire for more—more—that intense desire he had felt there in Lycurgus after Sondra came and now this, this! And now even this was ending—this—this— Why, he had scarcely lived at all as yet. . . . Oh, he really did not want to die. He did not. . . . Would no one ever understand?

The only real response to his unspoken plea for understanding is the narrative form in which that plea finds expression.

Technique especially emphasizes theme through the plot structure of book 3 of *An American Tragedy*. Dreiser's exhaustive presentation of the trial proceedings does not detract from, but rather, adds to the artistic power of the novel, for it amplifies the idea of society's subversion of selfhood in a particularly revealing way: by showing how facts and events already known to us as readers are discovered and described by "the world," Dreiser uses a superficial repetition of plot details to accentuate how *un*repetitious—how transformed—those details become when filtered through various minds all eager to do anything with Clyde *except* understand him. The re-creation of Clyde's past history by the legal authorities, the press, and the public dramatically illuminates society's indifference to and falsification of the meaning of his individuality. And in this manner, the last section of the story embodies an ironic commentary on the tragic meaning of the work as a whole.

When Dreiser withdraws his camera eye to a vast remove from Clyde at the start of book 3, after intensely involving us with him up close during much of book 2, one of the purposes of this manipulation of narrative distance is to suggest the dehumanizing distance from which Clyde is judged and dealt with by the community. In books 1 and 2 the fictional emphasis is upon the way Clyde's exploration of society and his status in it encourages him to counterfeit various versions of himself in order to be like, or liked by, others who seem "important." In book 3, conversely, the emphasis is upon the way society examines Clyde and his meaning to it through a ritualized reenactment (in reverse) of the same process of distortion: ironically, everyone now makes up versions of Clyde to suit their own needs, implicitly denying his individual importance. As Frederick Hoffman puts it, the public probes Clyde's actions and reaches conclusions about him without concerning itself with the experiential nature of his life: "He is doomed to die without any real exploration in depth of the terms of his having been victimized."

Having committed an ambiguous crime because of the ambiguity of his identity and prospects in Lycurgus, Clyde is tried and condemned by those who neither care about nor comprehend ambiguities, while the Wykeagy Avenue factors in his life vanish into apparent nonexistence. He discovers his dreams in the city and suffers their consequences in the country; his conduct is motivated by the ideals of urban sophistication and then judged by the provincial standards of rural religionism. Although he has no money, he is hated by the backwoods folk and their legal spokesman for being related to those who do; his own poverty prevents him from circumventing the law, and his uncle's wealth keeps him from pleading temporary insanity, the means of defense which his lawyers see as his only hope. District Attorney Mason assails Clyde for the ambitions that made him reject Roberta, but exploits Clyde's case in order to further his own political ambitions; Mason privately sees and ridicules Clyde's unintelligence and criminal ineptitude, but publicly denounces him as a cunning, vicious murderer. What the prosecution lacks in evidence to prove his guilt can be obscured in the tide of emotion against him stirred by Roberta's pathetic letters—which even unworldly Mrs. Griffiths knows make a fair trial impossible. And if they are unable to find unambiguous proof that Clyde murdered Roberta, Mason and "the people" are just as satisfied to be able to demonstrate his sexual transgression against her: Clyde is essentially condemned as "a rapist."

Like Tom and Daisy Buchanan in *The Great Gatsby*, the Lycurgus Griffiths and Finchleys show themselves to be "careless people . . . [who] [smash] up things and creatures and then [retreat] back into their money or their vast carelessness." Clyde's relatives and Sondra do everything possible to dissociate themselves from him and his trial, withdrawing to a safe distance into their respective cushioned purgatories in the Boston suburbs and at Narragansett. But their reactions to Clyde's "crime" and trial are less an indication of their individual callousness and "carelessness" than of their social class. For as Philip Gerber states, "Notwithstanding the distribution of guilt among the many, back of the scenes powerful forces, both economic and political, are at work determining who shall be exposed, who protected — and money and position are the major determinants." Ironically, that is, their power to command a separate standard of justice and to transcend common moral obligations to others permits the guilty rich to preserve their dignity as individuals while the innocent poor are being degraded. Clyde's mother, becoming a reporter and then a lecturer in order to pay her way to his trial and to finance his appeal, is treated as an object to be laughed at for her religiosity or to be "opened" impersonally, like a desk drawer, so that the public may have colorful information about "the murderer's" past and parents. Even the dead Roberta receives less respect than rich "Miss X," whose identity is fully protected: to borrow John McAleer's eloquent summary, "Those who would avenge her care nothing for her dignity as a person." This is shown as letters exposing Roberta's whole relationship with Clyde are sold as scandalous entertainment to the gruesomely gay crowd (along with hot dogs and peanuts), while, by contrast, Sondra's letters to Clyde are kept sacredly private — not even being admitted as evidence in the trial. The authorities consider it more important to minimize Sondra's exposure to shame than to maximize the jury's understanding of the reasons for Clyde's feelings and conduct. Likewise, Samuel Griffiths briefly wonders whether his neglectfulness toward his nephew contributed to the situation that led to Clyde's "crime," but would never consider appearing in court to state the exculpatory facts. He is principally preoccupied by the public strain that Clyde has brought upon the "Griffiths name," in the process endangering his children's positions as social luminaries.

Clyde's defense attorneys are no more prepared than the prosecutors or public to seek a true understanding of his character and conduct, and no less eager to manufacture a version of him conducive to their own purposes. Feeling that the truth is too ambiguous to win an acquittal for him, Belknap and Jephson create a pseudotruth implying a very different Clyde than the one who helplessly accepts their strategy. While Mason is portraying him as a fiend who killed Roberta even before she drowned, they are engaged in describing him as the youth whose "change of heart" about marrying Roberta made her "jump for joy," causing the boat accident on the lake in which she died. So after partly falsifying his identity just by understating "Miss X's" impact on his life, the defenders complete the process of inventing a Clyde who had decided to put duty before desire by giving her up and sacrificing his dreams for the sake of poor Roberta. Thus the trial is the ultimate form of Clyde's self-betrayal and betrayal by others: ironically, to try to save his life he must both suffer and support an implicit repudiation of the Ideal (personified by Sondra) that has been his *raison d'être*.

Condemned to die by a society indifferent to the meaning of his life, Clyde is put in solitary confinement (aptly symbolizing his whole way of being) in a penitentiary where he is stripped of all remaining signs of his identity but his very name. And while awaiting execution there, he reaches out for compassion and communion toward the only two people by whom he has not been abandoned. But it is sadly ironic that both of these people — a clergyman and his mother — are so dedicated to spiritual values that they are utterly incapable of understanding him no matter how intensely they sympathize with him. In his final days, Clyde turns to the Reverend McMillan in a desperate effort to understand *himself* and to be understood. Trying especially to settle the tormenting question of whether or not he is guilty of killing Roberta, he tells his spiritual adviser the entire truth about his life history and the event at Big Bittern, to the extent that he is able to grasp and articulate that truth. Yet this first and only sincere effort in his whole life to escape aloneness and make his true selfhood known to an Other, is doomed to failure. For while McMillan realizes that "never in his life" has he been confronted by "so intricate and elusive and strange a problem" as that of the prisoner's moral and legal guilt or innocence, the clergyman is compelled by his insistence on absolute truths to reach unambiguous conclusions. Having decided that Clyde's thoughts, if not his actions, were those of a murderer, McMillan fails to distinguish between his guilt before man and his guilt "before God" for what happened on the day of Roberta's death. Thus at the crucial moment during an interview with the governor of New York, the clergyman fails to mention all the extenuating circumstances in Clyde's crime — of which he alone is aware — to plead for commutation of the boy's death sentence to life imprisonment. Feebly declaring that he has "entered only upon the spiritual, not the legal aspect of [Clyde's] life," McMillan avoids a complex issue and walks away, though he will later be haunted by doubts: "Clyde's eyes! That look as he sank limply into that terrible chair . . . that confession! Had he decided truly — with the wisdom of God, as God gave him to see wisdom? Had he? Clyde's eyes!" And just before his death, Clyde is convinced to participate in a different sort of betrayal of the self, writing and signing a "Letter to the World" (how ironically named!) that urges all young men to lead Christian lives and aspire only to Jesus's love. Counterfeiting a "religious" Clyde, the boy holding the pen tries to be what he is asked to be by the reverend, one whose approval he seeks; working a new twist into the old thread of self-distortion, he becomes a grotesque parody of precisely the kind of "Clyde" he began his life by rejecting.

Although she pleads eloquently and emotionally for his life during the interview with the governor, Mrs. Griffiths does not even know her son as well as the clergyman does. For Clyde's sense of "how little, really, she had ever understood of his true moods and aspirations" prevents him from confessing to his mother all the facts and feelings he had told McMillan. Indeed, Clyde sees that it would be futile for him to explain to her the dreams that led to his "crime":

> It was as though there was an insurmountable wall or impenetrable barrier between them, built by the lack of understanding—for it was just that. She would never understand his craving for ease and luxury, for beauty, for love—his particular kind of love that went with show, pleasure, wealth, position, his eager and immutable aspirations and desires. She could not understand these things. She would look upon all of it as sin—evil, selfishness.

The failure in understanding that divides them is complete, for in her religious fanaticism (and extreme exclusion from the society that shaped his goals), Mrs. Griffiths categorically rejects all the values and viewpoints that have given meaning to Clyde's life. At the end of the novel, it is poignantly clear that the son for whom she weeps and prays never really existed for her *as an individual* in the first place.

Critical approaches to American literary naturalism have traditionally stressed the philosophical outlook, rather than the fictional composition, of works in this distinctive strain in the modern novel. Correspondingly, many critics have held Theodore Dreiser, whom they designate (and can thus dismiss) as the preeminent or at least prototypical naturalistic novelist, to be a powerful writer of remarkably scant craft. Yet as I have sought to suggest here, *An American Tragedy*, Dreiser's masterwork, manifests a complex interweaving of form and technique essential to its thematic content. In the story of Clyde Griffiths, the novelist implicitly articulates his profound concern about a materialistic society's subversion of the principle and dignity of selfhood. With irony and sorrow, Dreiser illuminates the nature of Clyde's betrayal by others and self-betrayal in the pursuit of illusions based on the belief that appearances are equivalent to essences. Thinking that *having* is the same as *being*, Clyde repudiates his own identity as meaningless and chases his dreams with a desperate selfishness ironically born of his need to become a self. And when he is led to plot the death of a poor girl to pursue marriage to his golden Ideal because frustrating social realities conflict with socially authorized dreams, the resultant "crime" he commits is fundamentally against himself: as his compulsive (and tell-tale) use of his own initials in the aliases of the murder plot hints, he ultimately loses himself while seeking his identity. What ensues from Clyde's ill-fated attempt to authenticate a self of Success is his isolation within a world that judges, without trying to truly understand, his individual story of failure. Expressing as well as emphasizing this theme, the novel's narrative techniques—its structural parallels between parts of the whole, its manipulations of point-of-view, and its closing section's symbolic commentary on the foregoing phases of the plot—indispensably infuse the book with meaning. And in the last analysis, fictional form in *An American Tragedy* is the figure in the carpet that allows us to grasp fully the "tragic" impact of Dreiser's art.

From Fact to Fiction:
An American Tragedy

Shelley Fisher Fishkin

In an essay called "Hey, Rub-a-Dub-Dub," published in 1917, Dreiser placed contrasting newspaper clippings side by side in a manner which caused them to clash in harsh cacophony; they could not possibly be reconciled into a meaningful whole. Dreiser's point, in the essay, is that life is simply too complicated to be unraveled. Throughout the essay runs the refrain that it is "all inexplicable," and that "all we know is that we cannot know." In a 1922 essay on "The Scope of Fiction" in the *New Republic* Dreiser voiced his doubts even more directly: "regardless of the realist or romanticist or the most painstaking dispenser of fact in science and history, I know by now that life may not be put down in its entirety even though we had at our command the sum of the arts and the resourcefulness of the master of artifice himself. There are, to begin with, suggestions and intimations just beyond the present scope of the senses that appear forever to elude us. And within the present range of human contact or report there is an immense body of fact that will not be penned. It is of a texture and substance that is beyond the palate and stomach of the race." Even at *Butterick's*, as a colleague recalls, "he was always searching, probing, thinking, delving down for facts, yet acutely conscious that one seldom achieved what one was after." Dreiser was not deterred by this problem, however, and it is responsible for whatever humility shines forth in his art. "He can entertain almost any idea and accept almost any experience," Robert Elias has observed, "so long as the idea or experience does not lay claim to exclusiveness" (preface to *Letters of Theodore Dreiser*).

From *From Fact to Fiction: An American Tragedy.* © 1985 by Shelley Fisher Fishkin. The Johns Hopkins University Press, Baltimore/London, 1985.

Dreiser's suspicions about the limitations inherent in his own fictions led him to form his greatest work, *An American Tragedy*, with peculiar openness and ambiguity (as we will show), as if he were unwilling to assume as narrator a claim to authority over the truth about his characters' lives. For in the end, Dreiser recognized that the role of the artist was not the role of someone who replaces stale and false explanations of life with new explanations soon to become equally stale and false. Rather, it was the role of someone able, in Dreiser's words, to "tear the veil from before [his readers'] eyes" by teaching them how to see on their own, as they had never seen before, the complex life that surrounds them.

This had not been Dreiser's goal as a fiction writer from the start. Indeed, his earliest efforts at fiction were characterized by extravagantly bizarre and outlandish settings that had absolutely nothing to do with the world he was documenting as a journalist. Dreiser's earliest creative effort was a preposterous comic opera in which an Indiana farmer was magically transported back to the Aztec empire where the shocked natives dubbed him their king. He never attempted to get "Jeremiah I" published. In the first story he did submit for publication the main character dreams he is an active participant in a vicious ant war, and is saved from death only by awakening to reality. Dreiser was incensed when *Century Magazine* rejected the story.

When his friend Arthur Henry prevailed upon him to start a novel in 1899, Dreiser made the key decision to place his characters (who were based on members of his family) in scenes he had witnessed and documented as a reporter. The breadlines, the railroad yards, the bustling city streets, the Broadway crowds, the factories, the luxury hotels that would appear in *Sister Carrie* were all familiar to Dreiser from direct observation. Two of his magazine articles, "Curious Shifts of the Poor," which appeared in *Demorest's*, and "Whence the Song," which appeared in *Harper's Weekly*, found their way into *Sister Carrie* with few revisions. Both *Sister Carrie*, and the novel that followed it in 1911, *Jennie Gerhardt* (which was similarly based on people and scenes Dreiser personally knew), forced readers to take a fresh look at some of their society's most accepted assumptions. As Swanberg has noted, the books that were selling when those novels appeared "were the glittering and virtuous costume romances, *When Knighthood Was in Flower, Janis Meredith, Soldier of Fortune*. Lust and vice were allowable only if punished in the end—as they had been in *McTeague*—to furnish the reader a wholesome moral lesson." In Dreiser's novels, however, transgression was presented with tolerance and understanding. Dreiser required his reader to accept, in Jennie Gerhardt's case, the seeming paradox of a virtuous sinner, and in Carrie's, of a successful one. Both images challenged the moral categories implicit in the popular novels of the day.

While Dreiser's profiles of successful businessmen for *Success* and other magazines may have sparked his interest in a businessman as a fruitful subject for a novel, he would incorporate only one of his magazine articles into his next novel, *The Financier* (the piece was "A Lesson from the Aquarium," published in *Tom Watson's Magazine*). Based on the life of financier Charles T. Yerkes, *The Financier* was heavily researched by Dreiser from newspaper files, books, interviews, and public documents. As Robert Penn Warren has observed, the novel's hero, Frank Cowperwood, "is not a fictional creation based on Yerkes; he is, insofar as Dreiser could make him, the image of Yerkes" (*Homage to Theodore Dreiser*). In addition to giving his reader an unprecedented inside view of the world of business and finance, Dreiser made Yerkes's life read like the epic poem of the predator-hero by allowing his grandeur and "soul-dignity" to shine through his often sleazy machinations. No conforming Babbitt, Frank Cowperwood came across as both sophisticated and (in his own way) honest. Even in prison he is, fundamentally, free. Yet while Frank Cowperwood may be, in one sense, freer than almost any character that had yet appeared in American literature, in another sense he was a peculiarly modern kind of slave. Dreiser titles the trilogy of Cowperwood books, of which *The Financier* was the first, a "Trilogy of Desire." As the title suggests, Cowperwood was enslaved by a desire which, like Carrie's, would always outstrip its attainments. In his dramatic portrayal of the amoral energy that inhered in the ever-reaching, overreaching desire of a Cowperwood, Dreiser shined a spotlight on an aspect of American life that had been largely absent from both literature and journalism despite the fact that it was the force which animated and dominated the age.

Dreiser would incorporate aspects of several of his magazine articles into *An American Tragedy*. A piece called "Pittsburgh" which he wrote for the *Bohemian* aptly prefigures the walks between the poor and wealthy parts of town that Clyde will take in the novel; a piece Dreiser published in 1910 on "The Factory" is a clear rehearsal for his fictional factory scenes; and the opening of an article called "The Man on the Bench" which Dreiser wrote for the *New York Call* distinctly foreshadows the opening lines of *An American Tragedy*. But Dreiser's initial interest in the subject that would form the core of the novel dates back to his days as a newspaperman in St. Louis.

"In so far as it is possible to explain the genesis of any creative idea, I shall be glad to tell you how *An American Tragedy* came to be," Dreiser wrote two years after the book was published, in response to an inquiry,

> I had long brooded upon the story, for it seemed to me not only
> to include every phase of our national life—politics, society,
> religion, business, sex—but it was a story so common to every

boy reared in the smaller towns of America. It seemed so truly a story of what life does to the individual — and how impotent the individual is against such forces. My purpose was not to moralize — God forbid — but to give, if possible, a background and a psychology of reality which would somehow explain, if not condone, how such murders happen — and they have happened with surprising frequency in America as long as I can remember.

Dreiser's personal familiarity with a murder like the one Clyde Griffiths would commit dates back to his days as a reporter for the *St. Louis Globe-Democrat.*

In 1892 Dreiser covered the story of a young perfume-dealer who murdered his pregnant sweetheart with poisoned candy. As he would later recall, in a magazine article,

It was in 1892, at which time I began work as a newspaperman, that I first began to observe a certain type of crime in the United States. It seemed to spring from the fact that almost every young person was possessed of an ingrowing ambition to be somebody financially and socially. In short, the general mental mood of America was directed toward escape from any form of poverty. This ambition did not imply merely the attainment of comfort and the wherewithal to make happy one's friends, but rather the accumulation of wealth implying power, social superiority, even social domination.

At this juncture in American history, Dreiser recalls, "Fortune-hunting became a disease," and the frequent result was what Dreiser came to view as a peculiarly American kind of crime.

In the main, as I can show by the records, it was the murder of a young girl by an ambitious young man. But not always. There were many forms of murder for money. . . . [One variation] was that of the young ambitious lover of some poorer girl, who in the earlier state of affairs had been attractive enough to satisfy him both in the matter of love and her social station. But nearly always with the passing of time and the growth of experience on the part of the youth, a more attractive girl with money or position appeared and he quickly discovered that he could no longer care for his first love. What produced this particular type of crime about which I am talking was the fact that it was not always possible to drop the first girl. What usually stood in the way was pregnancy, plus the genuine affection of the girl herself for her love, plus also her determination to hold him.

"These murders," Dreiser wrote, "based upon these facts and conditions, proved very common in my lifetime and my personal experience as a journalist."

From the time he began work as a journalist Dreiser collected clippings about young men who murdered (usually pregnant sweethearts) for social and economic advancement. While there are innumerable inconsistencies among Dreiser scholars regarding the specific cases Dreiser followed, there is evidence that Dreiser was familiar with at least ten murders of this sort, which took place in locales as varied as Missouri, New York, California, West Virginia, South Carolina, Massachusetts, and Illinois. Dreiser continued to collect clippings of this sort even after *An American Tragedy* was published; at one point he claimed that he knew of one crime of this nature that had taken place nearly every year between 1895 and 1935.

One such case interested him particularly when he came to New York to work on Pulitzer's *World* in 1894 and met the criminal's mother. Carlyle Harris, an "intern in one of the leading New York hospitals," seduced

> a young girl poorer and less distinguished than he was, or at least hoped to be. No sooner had he done this than the devil, or some anachronistic element in the very essence of life itself presented Carlyle with an attractive girl of a much higher station than his own, one who possessed not only beauty but wealth. The way Carlyle finally sought to rid himself of the other girl was to supply her with a dozen powders, four of which were poisoned, and so intended to bring about her death. One of them did. Result: discovery, trial and execution.

Dreiser became aware of another case while working as a magazine writer in New York in 1911. Clarence Richeson, a young preacher "with a small church in Hyannis,"

> had come up from nothing, learned little or nothing, accumulated no money, and was struggling along on a small salary. . . . From all I could gather at the time Avis was a charming and emotionally interesting and attractive girl, but of circumstance and parentage as unnoticed as [Richeson's]. Alas, love, a period of happiness, seduction with a promise of marriage, and then Mephistopheles, with nothing more and nothing less in his hand than a call to one of the richest and most socially distinguished congregations in Boston. There followed his installation as pastor, and soon after that one of the wealthy beauties in his new congregation fixed her eye on him and decided that he was the one for her. Yet in the background was Avis and her approaching motherhood. And

his promise of marriage. And so, since his new love moved him to visions of social grandeur far beyond his previous dreams he sought to cast off Avis. Yet she in love and agonized, insisted that he help rid herself of the child or marry her. Once more then, poisoned powders and death. And at last [Richeson] dragged from his grand pulpit to a prison cell. And then trial, and death in an electric chair.

Time and time again Dreiser saw history repeat itself.

As early as 1906 Dreiser confided to a friend that he wanted to write a book about a murder. By 1919, he had begun two separate novels dealing, respectively, with a murder in New York City and one in Hyannis, Massachusetts. It was not until 1920, however, that Dreiser decided on the case that deserved his fullest attention: the murder of Grace Brown by Chester Gillette in Herkimer County, New York, in 1906. The first time that he and others heard of the crime, Dreiser recalled,

was when the press in a small dispatch from Old Forge, a small town not far from Big Moose Lake, announced that a boy and girl who had come to Big Moose to spend a holiday had gone out in a boat and both had been drowned. An upturned boat, plus a floating straw hat, was found in a remote part of the lake. The lake was dragged and one body discovered and identified as that of Billy Brown. And then came news of the boy who had been seen with her. He was located as the guest of a smart camping party on one of the adjacent lakes and was none other than Chester Gillette, the nephew of a collar factory owner of Cortland. He was identified as the boy who had been with Billy Brown at the lake. Later still, because of a bundle of letters written by the girl and found in his room at Cortland, their love affair was disclosed, also the fact that she was pregnant, and was begging him to marry her.

Inevitably here, as in all the other cases of this sort Dreiser encountered, the newspaper account treated the facts of the case and the trial in the conventional manner. But there was another story which intrigued Dreiser: the story of why this story kept repeating itself, of why this tragic pattern recurred so frequently, and what made it so distinctively American.

Chester Gillette, whose fanatically religious parents had run a slum mission in the West, ran away from home at age fourteen and spent several years working at odd jobs across the country—printer's devil, merchant seaman, and brakeman. He spent two years at Oberlin College before meeting an uncle of his by accident in Illinois who offered him a job in his shirt factory in Cortland, New York. In Cortland Chester seduced Grace Brown, a girl who worked under him at the factory, who was the daughter of a poor South Otselic farmer. Her nickname was "Billy." When their affair began, Billy moved out of the home of the married sister with whom she had been living and rented a room of her own in another part of town.

During this period Chester had begun to advance in Cortland society and had become interested in a wealthy girl named Harriet Benedict, whom he knew only slightly, and who had not returned his love. Yet despite his discouragement, Chester was determined to achieve more status and material well-being than his alliance with Billy Brown could ever offer. When Billy announced her pregnancy, Chester insisted that she return to her parents and ignored her as long as he could. The pathetic letters she sent him from South Otselic moved the jurors to tears.

Unwilling to let Billy Brown hold him back from the prospect of a more comfortable and glamorous life, Chester enticed her into taking a trip with him, presumably to be married. In a rowboat at Big Moose Lake he brutally battered her head with a tennis racket and pushed her overboard. After she drowned, Chester left a straw hat he had bought for the occasion floating on the water to announce his own death. He fled the scene and was apprehended shortly and convicted. He was executed in the electric chair in March 1908, after an unsuccessful appeal.

Dreiser, working as a journalist in New York in 1906, had taken considerable interest in the stories about the Gillette case which he had read in the New York newspapers. The press devoted a great deal of space to every detail of the case, and Dreiser, like other readers, had the chance to learn many specific facts about both Gillette and his victim. The *New York World*'s artists had a heyday with the story as well, often filling a full quarter of the paper's front page (even more on inside pages) with drawings of "Chester Gillette as He Appears on Trial for His Life, and the Girl with Whose Murder He Is Charged," "Chester Gillette as He Appeared in Court and His Senior Counsel," and "Chester Gillette as He Appeared on the Witness Stand Telling His Version of Grace Brown's Death." In addition, the paper gave prominent play to photos, including a "Group Photograph of Gillette Family Taken When Chester Was Fifteen Years Old," one of the "Jurors Who Will Try Chester Gillette on Charge of Murder," and a picture of the "Prisoner's Handiwork in His Cell at Jail; Corner of Gillette's Parlor-like Cell, Decorated by Himself." It is no wonder that the heavily illustrated, sensational case made an impression on a writer who had been collecting clippings on crimes of this nature for years. Dreiser did not think about basing a novel on the case, however, until four or five years after he had read the newspaper accounts.

Ten years after *An American Tragedy* was published, Dreiser reflected in print on why he had been stirred by the case. "In my examination of such data as I could find in 1924 relating to the Chester Gillette-Billy Brown case," Dreiser wrote, "I had become convinced that there was an entire misunderstanding or perhaps I had better say non-apprehension, of the conditions or circumstances surrounding the victims of that murder *before* the murder was committed."

It was this "misunderstanding, or . . . non-apprehension," on the part of Americans, of the context in which the Gillette crime took place that helped prompt Dreiser to write *An American Tragedy*. The context in which the murder must be seen, Dreiser felt, was the fascination, shared by Americans across the nation, with the dream of rising through advantageous marriage from poverty to status and wealth. Versions of this dream had filled the pages of popular magazines Dreiser had encountered in his youth. The dream thrived in the consciousness of average people across America; and it underlay all of those chillingly similar crimes Dreiser had followed since the 1890s. And, almost without exception, it was viewed uncritically by the American public. Gillette, Dreiser wrote in 1935, *"was really doing the kind of thing which Americans should and would have said was the wise and moral thing to do* (attempting to rise socially through the heart) *had he not committed a murder."* Americans were blind, Dreiser felt, to important facts about themselves, their morality, their country, and their dreams. He wrote *An American Tragedy*, in large part, to help them take a fresh look at some of those facts.

While Dreiser departed from Gillette's story in his novel in several significant ways (as we will discuss), he kept extremely close to the record throughout much of the book. Both Chester and Clyde were the children of devout parents who had run a mission, and both came from the West to work for an uncle who had a factory in the East. The initials of the two boys are the same, and both begin affairs with poor farmers' daughters employed under them, who, as it happens, have similar nicknames (Grace Brown was called "Billy"; Roberta Alden was called "Bert"). While Grace's South Otselic becomes Roberta's "Biltz," the backgrounds of the two girls are nearly identical. In the novel Big Moose Lake, complete with its strange wier-wier birds, is changed, only in name, to "Big Bittern." Chester Gillette's tennis racket is changed to Clyde Griffiths's camera, but the trips planned by the two boys (save for the nature of the girls' deaths) are the same; both Chester Gillette and Clyde Griffiths use the pseudonym of "Carl Graham" during their travels.

The letters from Grace Brown which made jurors weep at the Gillette trial are extremely close to those which evoke the same pathos at the Griffiths trial:

(last letter from Grace Brown)	(last letter from Roberta Alden)
If you fail to keep your promise, Chester, to come to me Saturday, I will surely come to Cortland and you will have to see me there.	This is to tell you that unless I hear from you either by telephone or letter before noon, Friday, I shall be in Lycurgus that same night, and the world will know how you have treated me.

In the Gillette trial, the prosecutor states in his opening statement to the jury, "there was another person on the lake as they struggled, and when Grace Brown's death cry sounded over the water of Big Moose Lake this witness heard it. And she will be here." In the Griffiths trial in the novel, the prosecutor states in his opening statement to the jury, "as her last death cry rang out over the waters of Big Bittern, there was a witness, and before the prosecution has closed its case that witness will be here to tell you the story."

Newspaper reports of the Gillette trial say that "this announcement astounded the crowded, breathless courtroom as if the roof had fallen. Gillette, who had been watching the prosecutor speak without the slightest expression on his face, suddenly quailed, then straightened up in his chair and threw his head back." After the prosecutor's announcement in the novel, Dreiser writes, "the result was all that could be expected and more. For Clyde, who up to this time . . . had been seeking to face it all with an imperturbable look of patient innocence, now stiffened and then wilted. . . . His hands now gripped the sides of his chair and his head went back with a jerk as if from a powerful blow." At both the Gillette trial and the Griffiths trial, the round-bottomed rowboat and strands of the dead girl's hair are produced as evidence. Chester and Clyde each went through a forest after fleeing the lake, and each had the misfortune to meet three men who later testified against him.

Judge Devendorf's charge to the jury at the Gillette trial and Judge Oberwaltzer's charge at the Griffiths trial are nearly identical:

(Gillette trial)	(Griffiths trial)
"If any of the material	"If any of the material

facts of a case were at variance with the probability of guilt, it would be the duty of the jury to give the defendant the benefit of the doubt raised.	facts of the case are at variance with the probability of guilt, it would be the duty of you gentlemen to give the defendant the benefit of the doubt raised.
Gentlemen, evidence is not to be discredited or descried because it is circumstantial. It may often be more reliable evidence than direct evidence.	And it must be remembered that evidence is not to be discredited or descried because it is circumstantial. It may often be more reliable evidence than direct evidence.
While I do not say that you must agree upon your verdict, I would suggest that you ought not, any of you, place your minds in a position which will not yield if, after careful deliberation, you find you are wrong."	While I do not say that you must agree upon your verdict, I would suggest that you ought not, any of you, place your minds in a position which will not yield if after careful deliberation you find you are wrong."

A New York newspaper had reported Chester Gillette's reaction to the verdict as follows: "He leaned over a nearby table, he drew toward him a bit of white paper, and, taking a pencil from his pocket, wrote deliberately this message: 'Father, I am convicted. Chester.' It went to his father in Denver." Clyde Griffiths, in *An American Tragedy*, similarly, asking his lawyer "for a piece of paper and pencil . . . wrote: 'Mrs. Asa Griffiths, care of Star of Hope Mission, Denver, Col. Dear Mother—I am convicted. Clyde.' "

While no one knows the precise material relating to the Gillette trial to which Dreiser had access, it is clear from the above citations that Dreiser was familiar with at least the trial proceedings reported in the New York newspapers. He also had available a small pamphlet called "Grace Brown's Love Letters," which reprinted the letters Grace Brown sent to Chester Gillette in the early summer of 1906, shortly before her death.

In addition to doing extensive research in newspaper files, Dreiser personally visited the region of upstate New York where the Gillette crime had taken place. He collected vivid personal impressions of the drab and isolated farmhouses of South Otselic, of the sounds the birds made at Big Moose Lake, of the shape of the upstate woods to which Chester had fled. He visited a factory in Troy, New York. And he even took his cousin-consort Helen Richardson out in a rowboat on Big Moose Lake presumably to help him capture more authentically the crime that took place there. Dreiser also finagled his way into the death block at Sing Sing to get "the physical lay" of the place. (On this occasion—as, on others—Dreiser was less than overwhelmed by what he saw. He commented, about his visit there, "My imagination was better—(more true to the fact)—than what I saw.")

Before examining the ways in which Dreiser departed from the facts of the Gillette case in *An American Tragedy*, I would like to suggest some hypotheses as to why he stayed as close to them as he did.

One important reason was his conviction, reiterated throughout the book, that fact is fate. In all of the clippings Dreiser collected, the young murderer sought to eradicate the fact of his initial sexual transgression and the need for any responsibility for its consequences. But, repeatedly, fact would prove to be destiny; the young man's deeds and words would follow him regardless of the cleverness of his attempts to evade them.

In keeping with the pattern he observed in these crimes, Dreiser insists in *An American Tragedy*, that fact cannot be avoided; there is no turning away from the concrete events which shackle one's past to one's future. Clyde never really succeeds in running away from the automobile accident he had in Kansas City (it comes back to haunt him at his trial). He finds that ignoring Roberta does not make her (or the fact of her pregnancy) go away; neither does murdering her. The travel folders he bought, the photographs he took, the questions he asked, the letter Roberta wrote to her mother but had not had time to mail—all conspire to convict Clyde at his trial.

A second reason for staying close to the facts of the Gillette case in his novel was Dreiser's desire to make his story not merely an absorbing imaginative creation, but the story of America as well, at a particular juncture in its history. Dreiser wanted to document the time in which he lived; he wanted to synthesize what he saw as key aspects of the culture he had come to know since his childhood. He wanted to encompass in his novel "every phase of our national life—politics, society, religion, business, sex."

By rooting his book as firmly in actuality as he did, he could be more confident of achieving the referential power he wanted to achieve. He wanted the lakes and poor farmhouses to be the lakes and farmhouses of upstate New York. He wanted Roberta to *be* all of those poor country girls who came to work in factories in the nearest city. He wanted Clyde Griffiths to be all of those ill-fated young American boys who had committed similar crimes—and all those who might never commit crimes, but who shared his ambition, his insatiable cravings, his youth, optimism, and illusion.

Dreiser succeeded in giving his novel the referential power to which he aspired, both on the social and the individual level. As Robert Penn Warren has observed, one feels, in the novel,

> a historical moment, the moment of the Great Boom which climaxed the period from Grant to Coolidge, the half century in which the new America of industry and finance-capitalism was hardening into shape and its secret forces were emerging to dominate all life.

Dreiser himself proudly boasted of the letters he received from young men all over the country who saw portraits of themselves in Clyde Griffiths.

Dreiser's many minor changes in the Gillette story—such as his switching a shirt factory to a collar factory, changing a tennis racket to a camera, adding a local political battle to the trial—are useful and interesting, but the most important changes in *An American Tragedy* are: (1) the description of Clyde's character and background; (2) the description of American culture that emerges from the shared values of other invented characters in the novel; and (3) the description of the drowning. For it is through the first two of these elements that Dreiser succeeds in exposing as illusions some of the conventional assumptions and explanations which dominate American society. And it is through the last that he challenges the possibility of *any* completely adequate explanation of reality. By pointing up the inadequacies of this and any one version of reality, Dreiser forces the reader to "go back, in so far as we may, to the primary sources of thought, i.e., the visible scene, the actions and thoughts of people, the movements of Nature and its chemical and physical subtleties, in order to draw original and radical conclusions for ourselves."

Clyde Griffiths's background and character are very different from the background and character of Chester Gillette. Clyde's parents were poorer, and his childhood more circumscribed and deprived. Clyde was less scheming than Chester was. His formal education was inferior to that of his real-life model; he was less well-traveled and sophisticated. In many ways, as some critics have observed, he was more like Theodore Dreiser than he was like Chester Gillette.

He was also more like another American figure as well: the hero in a Horatio Alger novel. Dreiser knew the Alger novels well, having started reading them avidly at age ten. The plot of *An American Tragedy* up to the point when Clyde goes to Lycurgus—in other words, the portion of the book that relied most heavily on Dreiser's powers of invention—bears a striking resemblance to the standard Alger plot, as the chart below indicates. In many ways, of course, the young man Samuel Griffiths meets at the Union League Club is not at all like an Alger hero: he is selfish and weak and has not done anything specifically heroic. But even Alger heroes are known to have their faults; what counts is that Clyde's uncle *perceives* him as a youth characterized by those qualities typical of Alger heroes. Indeed, while not sparing the reader a view of Clyde's flaws, Dreiser emphasizes his virtues throughout the first part of the novel, making the resemblance between his own plot and the Alger plot even stronger. The plot summary of the typical Alger novel (in the column on the left) was constructed by Alger's most recent biographer [Gary Scharnhorst, in *Horatio Alger, Jr.*]; the plot summary on the right (my own) is that of *An American Tragedy:*

Alger's plot:

Dreiser's plot:

A teen-aged boy whose experience of the sinister adult world is slight, yet whose virtue entitles him to the reader's respect . . . enters the City, both a fabled land of opportunity and a potentially corrupting environment.

Clyde Griffiths, a teen-aged boy who knows little of the adult world but who is sensitive and thoughtful (if confused), and loyal to and respectful of his mother, gets a job at Kansas City's Green-Davidson Hotel, a place of great opportunity, and of potential corruption.

His exemplary struggle to maintain his social respect-ability, . . . to gain a measure of economic independence, . . . this is the substance of the standard Alger plot.

While Clyde's struggle is not "exemplary" (he leaves town when he is a passenger in a car that is involved in a hit-and-run accident), even Alger's heroes sometimes commit crimes in their youth for which they repent. Clyde is "terribly sorry" about the accident, and especially regrets the pain it caused his mother. He gets a series of solid, honest jobs, and sends money home whenever he can; he's determined to "make his own way as best he might" and rise above the

	oppressive poverty of his parents. He avoids the hotel business ("too high-flying, I guess"), and by chance (a contrivance common to Alger plots) he meets an old chum who helps him get a job at Chicago's Union League Club.
At length the hero earns the admiration of an adult patron who rewards him with elevated social station, usually a job or reunion with his patrician family, and the trappings of respectability.	As luck would have it (again an Algerism), Clyde's rich uncle turns up there. He is "obviously impressed" by Clyde's association with such a distinguished club, and also admires Clyde's neat appearance and "efficient and unobtrusive manners." Finding him bright and ambitious he offers him a job at his collar factory. The offer brings Clyde the standard Alger rewards listed at left: "elevated social station . . . reunion with his patrician family, and the trappings of respectability."

Clyde's fantasies, incidentally, when he gets a job at the Union League Club, resemble the fantasies of the millions of young people who, thinking to themselves, "this might happen to me," pushed Alger's novels into best-sellerdom:

> And who knows? What if he worked very steadily and made only the right sort of contacts and conducted himself with the greatest care here, one of those remarkable men whom he saw entering or departing from here might take a fancy to him and offer him a connection with something important somewhere, such as he had never had before, and that might lift him into a world such as he had never known.

(In addition, Clyde's fantasies of marrying Sondra are rooted in the "reality" of the world of Alger's heroes. The character of Sondra is nearly totally invented by Dreiser; there was no one like her in the Gillette case. However, in Alger's books there were many girls like her. As one of Alger's biographers described a familiar variety of female in an Alger novel, these wealthy young ladies "invited the hero to their homes for tea, and he took dancing lessons to acquit himself satisfactorily at their parties. But when they spoke to him, he fumbled for words; when they complimented him, he blushed." The hero usually ended up marrying such a girl—but implicitly, beyond the close of the book.)

While Alger always "abandoned his hero on the threshold of his good fortune, at the cultural boundary delimiting his place, rather than following him into that strange new world of opulence," Dreiser follows his hero into that "strange new world." He takes the remainder of his plot (from the point at which the Alger plot ends) from the story of the Gillette murder that appeared in the newspapers.

By merging the world of the Alger romance with the world reported in the daily newspaper, Dreiser forces his reader to see *both* texts in a new way. His strategy highlights the *incompleteness* of both the Alger plot *and* the newspaper story. The former ignores what happens to the young man after his fortunes are elevated; the latter ignores, for the most part, the early experiences that helped make him the way he is. The reader of the Alger story is not required to consider the repercussions of the hero's rapid rise; the formulaic structure of Alger plots encourages passive acceptance, on the part of the reader, of the author's "happily-ever-after" intimations. The reader of the newspaper story is similarly not required to become engaged with the material reported in more than a passive way; the young man described has already committed a crime, and, as a criminal, may be dismissed as a very different sort of person from the reader. Dreiser's strategy, however, produces very different results.

Dreiser lets the reader see Clyde's life through Clyde's own eyes in a way which evokes both sympathy and compassion. He lets the reader witness the parched and thirsting feelings Clyde has in the poor and musty rooms of his parents' mission, stifling in their bareness. And he lets the reader share Clyde's amazement at the luxury and comfort that surround him at the Green-Davidson Hotel. The reader has trouble condemning Clyde too harshly for allowing himself to be seduced by glitter and glamor.

Clyde is not perverse. He is not driven by any desires that are considered abnormal in society. He is not given to irrational outbursts; he is not even particularly passionate. He is a typical adolescent with typical adolescent "yearnings" and fantasies. He simply puts one foot in front of the other and suddenly finds himself tumbling down a mountainside from which there is no escape.

Telling Clyde's story the way he did, Dreiser challenged his readers' most unquestioned assumptions. The crimes Americans read about in the newspapers, in the 1890s, were "supposed to represent the false state of things, merely passing indecencies, accidental errors that did not count," Dreiser wrote. In short, crimes were considered curious aberrations from an otherwise good, honest, virtuous norm; and criminals were aberrant monsters whose exploits resembled those of beasts that had escaped from the zoo. In *An American Tragedy* Dreiser explores the *normality* underlying the criminal. And his notion forced his readers to take a fresh look at aspects of American life which they had grown accustomed to distorting or ignoring. While the reader of a Horatio Alger novel is soothed by the dream that anyone (including himself) can become a millionaire, the reader of *An American Tragedy* is disturbed by the nightmare that anyone (including himself) can become a murderer.

In exploring the normality underlying the criminal, Dreiser also dared to explore the criminality underlying the normal. The thirsting after wealth and respectability that motivated Clyde is identical to that which motivates other characters in the book, from all strata of American society. What separates them from Clyde is simply a matter of degree, not kind.

Hortense Briggs lies and schemes to get Clyde to buy her a new and expensive coat that is guaranteed to raise her social standing and hence her self-worth. (Meanwhile the coat-store proprietor lies and schemes to extract from her the maximum price.) Bella Griffiths tries to manipulate her father into building a bungalow at Twelfth Lake because she craves the status that summering there involves; she longs to be part of that set of families in Lycurgus that advertises its wealth and status with flashy cars, homes, and summer cottages. When simple shopgirls and the daughters of sophisticated factory owners are seen doggedly pursuing the same ends, the universality of these goals and of the often unsavory means these characters use to pursue their ends—lying, cheating, manipulating—is clearly established. There is a distinct aspect of criminality that underlies the normal throughout the book, and Dreiser constantly emphasizes it through such parallels.

The America portrayed in this novel is a grasping, greedy, and ever-thirsting culture that rarely, if ever, questions where it is going, or why. It is a society that accepts without question the validity of the American dream—the quest for success as defined by wealth and status. If his better-educated, higher-born compatriots have little reason to doubt the validity of striving for these goals, how can we expect Clyde to do so? For Clyde, as for most of the characters in the novel, "material success" was "a type of success that was almost without flaw, as he saw it."

While the reader is made aware of the multiple blemishes inherent in lives ruled solely by the dream of material success, Dreiser points out, evenhandedly, that such quests had valid aspects as well. For money solves many if not all problems in American society. Indeed, in American society as it is portrayed in the novel, money and status, in addition to providing comforts and glittering delights, can, in fact, get one out of almost any conceivable scrape.

Thus Belknap, one of the defense attorneys at Clyde's trial, had extricated himself as a young man from a problem similar to Clyde's with little difficulty. A college graduate who derived high social status from his father's position — "his father had been a judge as well as a national senator" — Belknap had run away from his problem as Clyde had, but without adverse consequences.

> In his twentieth year, [Belknap] had been trapped between two girls, with one of whom he was merely playing while being seriously in love with the other. And having seduced the first and being confronted with an engagement or flight, he had chosen flight. But not before laying the matter before his father, by whom he was advised to take a vacation, during which time the services of the family doctor were engaged with the result that for a thousand dollars and expenses necessary to house the pregnant girl in Utica, the father had finally extricated his son and made possible his return, and eventual marriage to the other girl.

In contrast to Belknap's easy solution, Clyde and Roberta are left to grapple with "the enormous handicaps imposed by ignorance, youth, poverty and fear." A doctor who was known to have performed an abortion for a girl "of a pretty good family" summarily refuses to have anything to do with a poverty-stricken girl like Roberta. Both of these episodes were invented by Dreiser to highlight a fact he did not want his reader to ignore. As he would later observe, looking back on Chester Gillette's plight, "you may depend upon it that if he had had money and more experience in the ways of immorality, he would have known ways and means of indulging himself in the relationship with Billy Brown without bringing upon himself the morally compulsive relation of prospective fatherhood."

In the society Dreiser documents in the novel, the pain and complexity of life's problems are constantly denied in favor of the "easy solution." Dreiser knew, however, that the easy solutions available to the rich were usually denied the poor. Despite the lip service America paid to the notion of equality, the poor were, for all practical purposes, treated as less equal than the rich. This reality (first encountered by Dreiser as a newspaper reporter) was denied by the roseate hues that permeated the pictures of American life that appeared in literature and by the rhetoric of politicians who trumpeted that all Americans were free and equal. But Dreiser was determined to prevent his reader from ignoring realities which popular fictions and rhetoric conspired to repress. It was vital to understand what money and status bought in America if one was to understand the manic acquisitiveness that ruled the day.

When Clyde first arrives in Lycurgus he walks down streets lined with elegant mansions and then reports for work at his uncle's factory. After work he strolls down River Street past more factories, and then he

> came finally upon a miserable slum, the like of which, small as it was, he had not seen outside of Chicago or Kansas City. He was so irritated and depressed by the poverty and social angularity and crudeness of it—all spelling but one thing, social misery, to him—that he at once retraced his steps and recrossing the Mohawk by a bridge farther west soon found himself in an area which was very different indeed—a region once more of just such homes as he had been admiring before he left for the factory.

Clyde continues to believe, throughout his life, that he can turn his back on poverty and deprivation as easily as he can retrace his steps out of this slum. The rich do it, after all. Why shouldn't he?

Embodying the "youth, optimism and illusion" that Dreiser felt characterized America as a whole, Clyde constantly assumes that there will be an easy way out of potential misery. His tragedy, in part, is the tragedy that stems from denying life its untidy complexity.

Clyde's catalog of problems and solutions reads almost like a parody of the advertisements that fill the magazines to which Dreiser contributed. Have you a pain? the ad would ask. Take our pill. Are you going bald? Use our cream. For Clyde, and for most of those around him, life itself seems filled with equally simple solutions. Poor? Get a job. In trouble with the law? Get a pseudonym in a new city for a fresh start. Caught in a rut? Find a rich uncle. Got a poor girl pregnant? Throw her overboard. Convicted for murder? Appeal. Appeal denied? Take Jesus. (This final "solution" brings one full circle to the hymn Clyde's family sings in chapter 1: "The love of Jesus save me whole,/The love of God my steps control.") Each of these "solutions," however, is obviously inadequate and unsatisfactory, though Clyde has neither the mental nor the moral resources to understand why. Like millions of other Americans whose follies Dreiser often criticized, Clyde had never learned to think for himself.

Clyde comes by his inadequate mental equipment naturally, through no fault of his own. His father, we learn, "poorly knit mentally as well as physically," was the "product of an environment and a religious theory, but with no guiding or mental insight of his own." His mother accepts without question the religious maxims that hang on her mission walls despite daily challenges to their wisdom. It is not surprising that Clyde lacks the mental and moral faculties to view his surroundings critically. He has been told all his life that he is free to choose the road to heaven or hell, and he assumes he is as free to choose success or failure, wealth or poverty, happiness or misery. He is unaware of the extent to which he is not free. Like so many other characters in the book, Clyde is bound up in a morass of illusions that impede his ability to deal effectively with the realities he encounters.

Dreiser is well aware of the inadequacy of Clyde's perspective on himself and his actions; for Dreiser knows that simplistic solutions, framed mottoes, and dreams of status and wealth fail to contain the complexities of life in the modern world. It is with stunning humility that Dreiser suggests that perhaps even a novel as long and dense and intricate as his may prove, in the end, to be equally incapable of containing those complexities.

Dreiser, willing to admit the possibility that some of the complexities which elude Clyde may elude him as well, makes the drowning of Roberta indeterminate and ambiguous, as if he were unwilling to assume authority as narrator over the truth about his characters' actions.

In the Gillette case, the murder was a rather straightforward one. There was clear evidence of heavy blows, obviously deliberate, upon the victim's face: "one whole side of her face had been bashed in, there had been brain damage from a three-inch gash behind her ear." Chester Gillette insisted throughout the trial that Grace Brown had committed suicide by jumping into the lake after he told her he would not marry her, but a physician who testified at the trial ruled out that possibility: "Dr. Edward Douglass testified that she was beaten over the head with a blunt instrument (such as a tennis racket) and that she was dead when she entered the water." There was clear evidence that Chester Gillette had murdered Grace Brown.

The evidence presented to the court in *An American Tragedy* is much more ambiguous. No "three-inch gash" announced that a brutal crime had been committed.

> While the joint report of the five doctors showed: "An injury to the mouth and nose; the top of the nose appears to have been slightly flattened, the lips swollen, one front tooth slightly loosened, and an abrasion of the mucous membrane with the lips"—all agreed that these injuries were by no means fatal.

Grace Brown's skull appeared to have been severely damaged by the heavy blows she received from the tennis racket; Roberta's head injuries, as well as the grasping position of her hands, however, indicated to the lawyers that Clyde's story about her having been hit in the head by the boat may have been true.

Strands of Grace Brown's hair which had stuck in the rowboat had been produced at the Gillette trial; one of the most incriminating pieces of evidence presented at Clyde Griffiths's trial is the bit of Roberta's hair supposedly found attached to Clyde's camera. But while there is no reason to doubt the authenticity of the hair exhibited at the Gillette trial, it is clear that the hair exhibited at the Griffiths trial was placed in the camera (some time after Roberta's death) by a morally overzealous backwoodsman named Burton Burleigh who desired to speed Clyde's conviction. The evidence that convicts Clyde Griffiths is thus, in part, more shadowy than that which convicted Chester Gillette.

The ambiguity of the evidence presented at Clyde's trial echoes the ambiguity of the events that took place in the rowboat. By a series of subtle maneuvers of syntax and diction, Dreiser manages to leave these events remarkably indeterminate, as we will show. The key sequence of events centering around Roberta's death occurs in the final five pages of book 2. These pages warrant a close examination. For here Dreiser shows himself to be more of a conscious stylist than he is credited with being. While Dreiser's literary career is spotted with innumerable instances of his insensitivity to the finer points of syntax and diction, in these pages he proves himself to be a master craftsman.

After an hour of rowing on Big Bittern, Clyde begins to experience the strange sensation that he, as well as the boat, is "drifting, drifting." Clyde is, indeed, drifting, emotionally as well as physically at this time, caught up in the flow of currents he does not fully understand. Dreiser evokes Clyde's passivity and lack of decision by narrating events through a shadowy fog of participial sentence fragments, passive constructions, static noun clusters, and other carefully chosen grammatical structures. In subtle ways, he inhibits the establishment of Clyde as an acting subject.

Shortly after Clyde feels this "drifting" sensation, he begins to drift grammatically through the narrative: "And suddenly becoming conscious that his courage, on which he had counted so much this long while to sustain him here, was leaving him, and he instantly and consciously plumbing the depths of his being in a vain search to recapture it." There is neither an active nor a passive verb in this "sentence" (which, from a syntactic standpoint, is not a sentence at all). One finds rather two drifting participial phrases connected by "and": (1) "becoming conscious that his courage . . . was leaving him, and he (2) . . . consciously plumbing the depths of his being."

One of several more standard constructions might have eliminated the "and" and changed "plumbing" to "plumbed," thus connecting these two phrases into a sentence. But Dreiser fractures his grammar consciously and not accidentally. For while a normal sentence structure might make Clyde the subject of an active verb (he . . . plumbed), Dreiser's floating participles allow Clyde simply to find himself in a state of doing something, set adrift in that state by forces beyond his awareness and control.

The pages following this passage are filled with many analogous examples of such "floating participles." By this term we mean participial phrases cut off from the larger sentences of which they would normally be a part and set adrift on their own. (They are not "dangling participles" since they correctly modify the nouns to which they implicitly or explicitly refer.) In the following passage, the participles italicized for easy identification are those which have Clyde alone as their subject:

> And Clyde, instantly *sensing* the profoundness of his own failure, his own cowardice or inadequateness for such an occasion, as instantly *yielding* to a tide of submerged hate, not only for himself, but Roberta—her power—or that of life to restrain him in this way. And yet *fearing* to act in any way—*being unwilling* to—*being willing* only to say that never, never would he marry her—that never, even should she expose him, would he leave here with her to marry her—that he was in love with Sondra and would cling only to her—and yet not *being able* to say that even. But angry and confused and *glowering*. And then, as she drew near him, seeking to take his hand in hers and the camera from him in order to put it in the boat, he *flinging* out at her, but not even then with any intention to do other than free himself of her—her touch—her pleading—consoling sympathy—her presence forever—God!

> Yet (the camera still unconsciously held tight) *pushing* at her with so much vehemence as not only to strike her lips and nose and chin with it, but to throw her back sidewise toward the left wale which caused the boat to careen to the very water's edge. And then he, stirred by her sharp scream, (as much due to the lurch of the boat, as the cut on her nose and lip), *rising* and *reaching* half to assist or recapture her and half to apologize for the unintended blow—yet *in doing so* completely *capsizing* the boat— himself and Roberta being as instantly thrown into the water.

Thus Clyde does not fling, push, reach, or capsize; rather, he somehow finds himself flinging, pushing, reaching, capsizing. The difference is vital.

Dreiser further intensifies Clyde's passivity by moving, in the final phrases of this passage, from active present participle ("rising" and "reaching") to passive present participle ("being thrown"). There are a number of other passive constructions in these pages, as well, many of which contribute directly to the ambiguity of Clyde's responsibility. Thus Dreiser refers to the moment of contemplated murder as "the moment [Clyde] or something had planned for him," rather than referring to the moment Clyde had planned; Clyde is the passive recipient here, of his own former plans, or of the plans of some force outside himself. After Roberta falls into the water, a voice at Clyde's ear tells him, "this—has been done for you"; again, it does not say, "this you have done."

The static nature of this important scene is established, in part, by Dreiser's direct references to "a static between a powerful compulsion to do and yet not to do," and to "the stillness of his position, the balanced immobility of the mood." But Dreiser also evokes stasis by frequently pasting noun clusters on the page, cut off from any verbs, active or passive: "the weird, haunting cry of that unearthly bird again," "His wet, damp, nervous hands!," "A sudden palsy of the will" are all treated as if they were sentences. These and the many disconnected images that appear in these pages help evoke a "weird" tableau of "balanced immobility."

On those few occasions in these pages when Dreiser does employ complete sentences and not sentence fragments, he almost always makes statements indicating necessity, possibility, or a future state—and not actions actually taken. These statements involve the words "would," "could," "might," "must," "needed to." For example, Dreiser writes, "All that [Clyde] needed to do now was to turn swiftly and savagely to one side or the other . . . It could be done—it could be done." But indicating the possibility of completing an action is very different from saying that that action has been completed. Again, Clyde has "done" nothing.

Clyde himself is unsure of the role he has played in Roberta's death. She sinks for the final time not after he has decided not to save her, but as he floats in his interminable indecision. "Had he [killed her]? Or, had he not?" Clyde ponders. From the moment Clyde is seen "becoming conscious that his courage . . . was leaving him" to the end of book 2, he ceases to be the subject of any active verb. Clyde's thoughts flow in sentence fragments and images. The reader sees him *in the process* of doing things (consciously or unconsciously), yet unaware of how he came to be doing them.

In a final effort to evoke the murkiness of the scene he relates, Dreiser constructs several masterfully ambiguous phrases. Dreiser shows Clyde "rising and reaching half to assist or recapture" Roberta when she falls into the water. The word "recapture" suggests that she is his captive; "assisting" (implicitly to save) and "recapturing" (implicitly to be able to destroy her himself) are thus polarly charged words, and the meaning of the sentence is ambiguous. Dreiser also refers to the blow Clyde "had so accidentally and all but unconsciously administered." Clyde's action was not completely unconscious; does this mean that it was somewhat conscious? Can something be *somewhat* conscious? If an action is somewhat conscious, can it also be accidental? The answers to these questions remain as clear as the silt on the bottom of Big Bittern.

Throughout *An American Tragedy*, as we have indicated earlier, Dreiser suggests the limitations of Clyde's outlook on life. But when it comes to the death of Roberta, the reader has no reason to believe that Dreiser knows more than Clyde does. Dreiser, supremely humble as an author despite his often pompous pride as a man, prefers to remain at Clyde's side, in the dark waters of his confusion, leaving the reader to postulate an explanation of the events on his own from the ambiguous cues offered.

Few writers of fiction have elicited the amount of literal reader participation that Dreiser elicited in this volume. The opinions of readers as to what "really happened" in the rowboat were so strong and diverse that Boni and Liveright decided to capitalize on them by running a contest. The essay contest they ran, on the topic, "Was Clyde Griffiths Guilty of Murder in the First Degree?," drew hundreds of entries from readers across the country and was eventually won by a law professor in Virginia. Because of the special openness and ambiguity with which Dreiser narrated the death of Roberta, readers were attracted to the idea of constructing interpretations of the event on their own.

Dreiser himself, in *An American Tragedy*, seemed to be unwilling to assume authority as narrator over what really happened to Clyde because he knew the complex facts of the event were unlikely to yield to any simple explanation. He preferred to admit that even he, as narrator, could not capture the "truth" about his characters, that they, like "the actuality of life," were

> A shadow
> That eludes one—
> Escaping by a thousand ways.

And rather than end his novel with the kind of resonant finality that is the novelist's prerogative, Dreiser chose to leave *An American Tragedy* peculiarly open-ended. In his final chapter Dreiser circles back to the words with which the novel began: "Dusk, of a summer night"; he then proceeds to begin the story of Russell (the child of Clyde's sister), who is being raised by Clyde's parents, and who is likely to relive, in his own way, Clyde's story. Implicit in this strategy is Dreiser's admission of the limitations of his novel: it contains the story of Clyde—but also of Russell? His final chapter reflects his belief that even a text as panoramic and dense as this one is destined to be incomplete, that life (and the experiences, tragedies, dreams, and mysteries it entails) resists containment in the writer's forms.

The Life History of Objects: The Naturalist Novel and The City

Philip Fisher

The opening scene of *An American Tragedy* leaps into new territory of the self in as striking and profound a way as the scene of the *petite madeleine* in Proust. A seedy little band is walking the streets, perhaps a family, but not enacting themselves as family. They are "the man-in-the-street," omitted in the attention of others who, likewise walking, scan or muse in the way one does as a "passerby" in the absence of events that solicit attention. Suddenly the band stops, two adults, four children. This is nowhere, no place. Suddenly it is a place they make up as they begin to sing. Now it is an improvised church, on the spot, and in singing they become ministers and choir, the passerby, their attention now solicited, must choose to become or refuse to be the congregation, audience, members of this half-hour church. In the middle of nowhere they have improvised a world, temporary, voluntary (only they accredit themselves "ministers," each person in the congregation is a self-appointed instant member of this church). On the spot a social structure exists with roles and tactics forced into existence under what seems emergency conditions: as someone might decree, "For tonight this square of sidewalk is my bed," or as someone can find himself in a storm and transform what was a moment before "newspaper" into "umbrella."

This fragile, ad hoc world transforms itself again, now into a business. The congregation is asked for money, is sold tracts. This is, after all, how these people get their living. Now each one in the congregation must contribute or refuse to "support" these people. The half-hour service ends, the congregation transforms itself into walkers by drifting away, becoming "the man-in-the-street." The ministers and choir move on, becoming walkers.

From *Hard Facts: Setting and Form in the American Novel.* © 1985 by Oxford University Press.

127

The place becomes nowhere, no place again. No trace, no "evidence" as the book will later name all traces of the past, remains. The experience, the roles, the physical reality of the church within which each lived for half an hour, dissolve.

No role exists unless it is honored like paper money in the eyes of others who must, in order to validate my role, not simply approve or permit, but enact a complementary role. They must become co-performers. If all passersby lower their eyes and walk on when a man begins to preach in the streets, they rule by their coperformance that he is performing the role of madman, not that of minister. Without the coperformers no one is anything at all. They are passersby.

The tactics for being someone under emergency conditions, conditions that are permanently temporary, fragile, improvised (without any prestructuring past), and absolutely dependent on the cooperative enactment of others, these are the essential tactics of identity in the city world of *An American Tragedy* or *Sister Carrie* where the profession of actress names this general condition precisely.

In choosing to begin with Clyde "in place," performing, but resentful of a squalid, theatrical self-enactment, Dreiser abandons the comforting sentimentality of the innocent central character. Typically, the novel of adolescence depends on an outsider who sees such structures first as an observer, then makes up himself by choosing among them. Such outsiders have a self that they invest with social position, career, and wife, usually in ways that express or publicize the nature of that self. In Dreiser no outsider exists, no innocent. Clyde begins in state, experiencing what was for Nietzsche the characteristic feeling of Western civilization—resentment. Every motion of his life compounds flight and desire, neither feeling exists even for a moment except in the presence of the other. As the motion of desire is given in the metaphor of shopping, so its opposite is generated literally with more and more overt force in the book; Clyde flees his family (metaphorically); he runs from the auto accident (literally); after the murder he becomes a fugitive (totally absorbed in flight).

Bluntly put, within Dreiser's novel the question of authenticity never exists. Clyde has no self to which he might be "true." Literally, he is not yet anyone at all. For the calm or even frantic possession of himself Clyde substitutes an alertness to the moods of others, to their "take" of him. By the end of the book the lawyer's projection of the jurors' take, designs every gesture Clyde will make. Ultimately, Clyde lives in their moods, borrows their being, as he had earlier borrowed Gilbert's appearance, until we have to say he is more often them than himself. So attentive is he to his observer that he springs to life as a reflection of what the observer appears to have seen. He gets his "self" moment by moment as a gift from the outside. He murders by imitation (after reading of a drowning in the newspaper) as he loves by imitation (his being mistaken for Gilbert).

Throughout the novel Clyde is in motion towards or away from worlds he does not merge with. Fleeing or yearning, running or shopping, seducing or aborting, saving money to buy, planning to do, hoping for—"if" and "if only," "could he only . . .": Dreiser begins hundreds of sentences with these words. The two motions to embrace and to murder, possess and amputate are sharpened and magnified by the staircase plot. With each turn the circumstance is wider, the matter more ultimate, but the same matters are, with each new circle, once again in view. Finally, at the same lake he seems ready at once to snatch at the social world he most desires and annihilate the clinging world from which he cannot be free.

Nowhere in Dreiser's novel is there the slightest trace of society, as that word is understood in nineteenth-century novels. Instead there are worlds, like the world of the Green-Davidson Hotel, the social world of the Griffiths, the world of condemned prisoners at the penitentiary, the shabby rural world Roberta comes from, the sexually languid world of the girls who work for Clyde. These worlds are islands of varieties of aura, some glamorous, some contaminating. Everyone in Mrs. Braley's rooming house appears to Clyde to be from "the basement world." He speaks of the "better atmosphere" of the Union Club in Chicago. No distinction expresses the fact that whereas he *lives* in the rooming house, he was a servant in the Union Club. The atmosphere soaks in equally. In the city all aura is translated into places, and the moments of entering a new atmosphere, whether of the restaurant the bellboys visit on their night off, the living room of the Griffiths mansion, the death row, or the dyeing room of the factory—these are among the most perfectly crafted moments of Dreiser's novel. Places supplant manners. In communities, in societies, manners were the codes of behavior, often most precise in speech and language, encoding deference or intimacy, reserve, assumption or condescension—codes of behavior that enact the rules of presence, the way in which we enter or situate ourselves in each other's experience. Places in Dreiser give out this social grammar once located in behavior, in manners, in the implications of conduct.

Zola was the first to abandon society as the object of public representation for the new post-social topic of "worlds." However, in Zola these islands have economic and systematic integrity based on work: the entire world of the coal mines in *Germinal,* the world of land and farming in *La Terre,* the military world of *Le Débâcle.* Each is a rational sector of experience, known by the array of types, the kinds of language or experience, the appropriate modes of sexuality, humor, pride, and violence. Public, permanent compartments of society, they imply the larger, total society even while the magnification Zola applies, the isolation of spheres, makes them seem absolute. The food world, the art world, the sex world of *Nana* are all paradoxically still within a world, although courtesan, artist, grocer are monomaniacally absorbed in their sectors of work.

For Dreiser the worlds are neither economic, nor public, nor are they permanent centers of activity. Worlds are not generated by the webs of work, because in Dreiser work itself is only one kind of atmosphere, enthralling to the bellboy of the Green-Davidson Hotel, contaminating to the worker in the "basement world" of the collar factory. Work is just another place where one is seen by others and fixed by their looks that melt self and atmosphere together. Dreiser's worlds are temporary, magical improvisations like the little religious world on the street, or the perfectly named "Now and Then Club" through which Sondra engineers her flirtation with Clyde and his entry into the social set. Every boarding house is a world, the hotel bellboys have their own world of nights out at restaurants and brothels or outings in the country. Even the condemned man, Clyde, and his two guards on the trip to Auburn prison make up a world performing itself for the crowds who gather to see the now-romantic murderer. The guards feel honored and proud (as Clyde once felt walking with Hortense) to be seen with the murderer. His aura gives them identity: they are "the murderer's guards" with a genitive construction as potent as the erotic genitive Clyde feels for "his beloved's breasts." Murderer and guards form one aural body as Clyde working at the Green-Davidson is a limb of one aural body that includes guests, employees, furniture, renown, position in St. Louis, and lights.

So many fragile, transient worlds exist in Dreiser's novel because the root meaning of world here is anything outside the body that, if seen by another, contaminates or glamorizes the self. When Clyde walks with Hortense she decorates him, testifies to him. Two lines of energy contribute to the power of worlds to share being, to lend identity: the first is the force of collective identity, the second, the magic of places.

Collective identity in the novel is more substantial than individual identity. Being "one of" the Griffiths or "one of" the Green-Davidson bellboys or "one of" the prisoners condemned to death, is a more precise matter than being Asa Griffiths or Ratterer or even Clyde Griffiths. The novel describes "sets" or bands, clubs or cliques. Many of the sharpest representations in the book are of days Clyde spends within a precise identity set. Dreiser brilliantly records the life of groups, factory workers moving through the streets to work, or the camping trip of the social set. He is remarkably indifferent to kinds of life that cannot be described as ongoing—activities or groups that one "joins."

Experiencing oneself as "one of" this or "one of" that is the primary way of constituting a self in the novel. The material is outside the body in sets. "He felt he would like to caress her arm. . . . Yet here he was a Griffiths—a Lycurgus Griffiths—and that was what now made a difference— that made all those girls at this church social seem so much more interested in him and friendly." Or again: "He danced with her and fondled her in a daring and aggressive fashion, yet thinking as he did so, 'But this is not what I should be doing either, is it? This is Lycurgus. I am a Griffiths here. I know how these people feel toward me.' " The perfect concision of identity: I am a Griffiths, *Here*. I am a bellboy, here. I am a condemned prisoner, here. These are the absolute figures of identity: collective and limited by that terrible word *Here*. Both set and setting are around the self. Dreiser notes that the old death row was literally a row with all the cells side by side so that the prisoners never saw one another, never saw the "Them" that each was "one of." In the new death row—to Clyde's fastidious distaste—the cells face and the men become a hysterical, visible set acting out in front of each other variations of their common fate and identity. Architecturally, the state of New York has taken account of the new conditions of self by making the setting enforce a set.

The first act of looking at someone in the book is to look *around* him. Clyde feels humiliated to know that as the eyes of others come to focus on him in the street the "around" that they notice first is the shabby religious family that he must wear like an irritating garment. Because the savor of worlds replaces the savor of individual character within the body, Dreiser designs a web of metaphors to represent this new condition. Clyde often wears a uniform, the first metaphor of "set" identity. First as a bellboy, later as a servant at the Union Club, then as a businessman, finally as a prison inmate. Uniforms designate both sets and one specific place within a setting, as in a resort hotel the casual clothes of the guests define their places, the formal uniforms of the elevator operators, theirs.

More profound than uniforms is the territory Dreiser calls "manner," a stylized, collective tone of behavior. After a time in the Union Club, Clyde, though a servant, takes on the aloof, sexless manner of the successful businessmen there. Manner is absorbed, not learned. The power of adopting a manner depends on an interior blankness over which many colorations can pass. In court Clyde's attorneys coach him in a manner, and when shaken he must look to the eyes of his lawyer whose return look will recall him to what he is supposed to be.

A more brilliant device of collective identity than either uniforms or

manner is the resemblance between Clyde and his cousin Gilbert. The blur
between the two identities creates the entire plot of the novel. Because Clyde
has the manner of the Union Club and is first seen by his uncle Samuel within its
civilized aura, and because he resembles in a striking way the manufacturer's
son Gilbert—a double "rented" being—he is invited to Lycurgus and given
a job. Again, Sondra Finchley offers a ride to Clyde, having mistaken him
for Gilbert; then begins her flirtation with him and opens society to him.
She continues, at first, only to irk Gilbert, to strike at Gilbert by taking
up his neglected cousin. It is only because he can so easily be "taken for"
someone else that Clyde can exist in Lycurgus as "himself."

Identity, blurred or collective, externalizes the question of who I am,
converts it into the question, Who do they take me for? Who does it look
like I am to them? A stunning scene enacted again and again in the book
could be called "looking around to see who I am." At the collar factory Clyde
approaches the secretary guarding the door.

> "Well?" she called as Clyde appeared.
> "I want to see Mr. Gilbert Griffiths," Clyde began a little
> nervously.
> "What about?"
> "Well, you see, I'm his cousin. Clyde Griffiths is my name.
> I have a letter here from my uncle, Mr. Samuel Griffiths. He'll
> see me, I think."
> As he laid the letter before her, he noticed that her quite severe
> and decidedly indifferent expression changed and became not so
> much friendly as awed.

After his capture people come to see him and he sees himself in their eyes:

> Their eyes showed the astonishment, disgust, suspicion or horror
> with which his assumed crime had filled them. Yet even in the
> face of that, having one type of interest and even sycophantic pride
> in his presence here. For was he not a Griffiths—a member of
> the well-known social group of the big central cities to the south
> of here.

Dressed as a prisoner, his hair cut, he sees himself as others might:

> There was no mirror here—or anywhere—but no matter—he could
> feel how he looked. This baggy coat and trousers and this striped
> cap. He threw it hopelessly to the floor. For but an hour before
> he had been clothed in a decent suit and shirt and tie and shoes,
> and his appearance neat and pleasing, as he himself had thought

as he left Bridgeburg. But now—how must he look? And tomorrow his mother would be coming—and later Jephson, or Belknap, maybe. God!

But worse—there, in that cell directly opposite him, a sallow and emaciated and sinister-looking Chinaman in a suit exactly like his own, who had come to the bars of his door and was looking out of inscrutable slant eyes, but as immediately turning and scratching himself—vermin, maybe, as Clyde immediately feared. There had been bedbugs at Bridgeburg.

A Chinese murderer. For was not this the death house? But as good as himself here. And with a garb like his own. Thank God visitors were probably not many.

A magnificent scene. Dreiser at a moment like this has no equal. Clyde imagines the "other" and then finds him out there as another version of himself. The Chinaman is the first installment of his "set" which he accepts by reminding himself: that's what I am *here*, in this setting. He ends grateful to be invisible. In miniature this scene recapitulates the curve of the book, and its sinister constituting glance that destroys, the glance of the Chinaman, is the world glance returned when Clyde looks around to see who "I" am.

On the street singing hymns he is wounded by "who" the bystanders take him to be. In court the eyes of the jury take him to be a murderer. The sexually vital girls he meets at the church social take him to be a Griffiths, and Clyde knows well the difference between being taken to be one of the Kansas City Griffiths and one of the Lycurgus Griffiths. Contaminated or magically ennobled, in either direction he is a blank center engulfed by worlds.

Often the aura of a world is precisely located in a building, a space that becomes a metonymy for that world. The Green-Davidson Hotel in Kansas City where Clyde works as a bellboy is evoked with rapture and desire. The hotel has more being, more reality than anyone within it. To each it rents out a part of its self so that the pale creatures become "someone who works at the Green-Davidson" or "someone staying at the Green-Davidson." Clyde looks at the Alden farm or the Griffiths mansion and sees them as "selves," as what could be taken for his self by others were he within. He shudders or feels exhilarated, threatened, or tempted by them in that intimate way most people feel only about *actions*. We feel honored or shamed by what we have done because, in our sense of self, what we *do* expresses and announces what we are. It is the one transmission from the portable, interior self. In Dreiser, this decisive burden of *actions* is taken over by settings. The two fundamental settings are clothes and the slightly larger garments that we wear called houses or rooms. Both are the first elements of the self around the body. The Griffiths' factory makes collars, an article of clothing. All of Clyde's money goes into clothes, a more widely visible self than one's room or house which one must leave behind much of the day. Decisive clues against him at his trial are his two straw hats, his clothes and suitcase. Hortense offers to exchange sex for a coat, and in one of the greatest of Dreiser's scenes, Clyde goes in desperation to a clothing store to learn from a clerk selling him ties where he can locate an abortionist.

Clyde is never intimately sculptured by his actions. He does not seem to do them. Every decisive event in his life is an accident, a mistake, or a confusion. In the existential sense, he does not "do" his life. For that reason his acts are not essential to who he is. He seems peculiarly absent at the most decisive moments, such as when an auto accident kills a child. To Clyde, Roberta dies by accident, really, and what was he in the boat but "someone" holding the camera she bumped her head against? He does not participate in what he does, but he does participate in where he is. These places index who we must take him to be, and they can be found outside him, while the accidental moral life of his acts goes its irrelevant way within. Being here and not there has replaced doing this and not that.

As a pun the word "place" suggests physical space, social station, and occupation at the same time. But for all the desperate importance of worlds and places within worlds, Clyde is never seen at home. He seeks admission or flees confinement, he desires and flees; worldless. The two haunted spaces of the novel where Clyde enacts his life are hotels and water. He begins work in a hotel, lives in the small-scale hotels that are rooming houses, finishes his life in the state-run hotel known as a prison. His outing with the bellboys and Hortense takes them to a hotel in the country, and before Roberta's death they go from hotel to hotel in the resort area. A hotel is an ideal home, like the street church with which the book begins, for improvised, over-night worlds.

Yet hotels *are* worlds. The Green-Davidson in Kansas City has a dense, alluring presence in spite of its changing cast. Dreiser can sketch in precisely the "world" of each of the rooming houses Clyde lives in — their manner, their tone, their place in the scale of society. Because they are worlds there exists a kind of visual rule to judge who does or does not belong there: who is, as we say, "out of place" there. The acute vision of the book does not rest with situating Clyde in transient, improvised worlds, temporary worlds, but in representing him as fundamentally worldless, unable to "belong there" even in temporary worlds. At the end he is dead, not of justice, nor of social revenge, but of a new disease: worldliness.

Within every world there are defective positions, reserved for those who are deeply "out of place" there, who don't belong, but are permitted to be on the spot if they agree to admit in some clearly announced way that their case is an exemption. The servants at the Union Club are poor boys permitted to bask in the aura of the club, sharing its dignified manner, treated with the civility of all relations there, even to be seen as part of this world—as Clyde is first seen by his uncle Samuel—but at the cost of signifying by their uniforms that they are there by permission and don't in fact belong. They participate in aura without membership in the world. This is Clyde's social place at every moment in the book. When invited to the Griffiths' mansion he can come only at the cost of their constant reminders that he is a poor cousin, there on tolerance as an act of kindness. In the social set that he cannot affort Sondra slips him seventy-five dollars so he can pretend to pay their way, and the money itself is his stigma. Even when he descends to a world, in the menial work of the factory, he is seen there as exempt since, as the nephew of the owner, he may suddenly no longer be a fellow worker but a boss. With the Griffiths set he is an outsider, but in every other set he is equally an outsider because the others see him as a Griffiths. Every world is doubled by his presence inside it.

On his first day at the Green-Davidson Hotel Clyde is called to room 529.

> [He was then . . .] sent to the bar for drinks . . . and this by a group of smartly dressed young men and girls who were laughing and chatting in the room, one of whom opened the door just wide enough to instruct him as to what was wanted. But because of a mirror over the mantel, he could see the party and one pretty girl in a white suit and cap, sitting on the edge of a chair in which reclined a young man who had his arm around her.
>
> Clyde stared, even while pretending not to. And in his state of mind, this sight was like looking through the gates of paradise. Here were young fellows and girls in this room, not so much older than himself, laughing and talking and drinking even.

Clyde sees the scene of youths like himself but mysteriously different, privileged, worlded, but he sees it in a mirror glimpsed through a crack in a door someone holds almost closed against him. His uniform and purpose there are the distance for which the slightly open door is a metonymy. He sees only an image, a fiction in the mirror. Later in the novel, the newspaper is this mirror. Clyde, with touching innocence, tells Sondra he has been following the social life of her set "in the newspaper." He reads in the newspaper of a drowning at a lake that gives him, in his empty resentment of Roberta, a crime that he can imitate. And in a stroke of grotesque brilliance, Dreiser has Clyde's mother support her trip east by acting as a reporter for a newspaper, writing up the sentencing to death of her own son!

The newspaper or mirror is a periscope in the novel, feeding images from worlds to other worlds. The newspaper is a metonymy for the world hunger Dreiser associates with the city, the torment of proximate worlds that one can never enter, turned into a self-torment by reading about even more fantastic, unavailable worlds.

Clyde enters always with a talisman or trick that simultaneously admits him and curses him: his uniform gives him the glimpses of the hotel paradise, his resemblance to Gilbert tickets his entry to Sondra and her set, the slipped seventy-five dollars pays his way into the camping vacation.

The most perfectly orchestrated scene of defective membership that marks Clyde throughout is his joining the campers after the murder of Roberta.

> For although met by Sondra, as well as Bertine, at the door of the Cranston lodge, and shown by them to the room he was to occupy, he could not help but contrast every present delight here with the danger of his immediate and complete destruction. . . .
>
> If only all went well, now, — nothing were traced to him! A clear path! A marvelous future! Her beauty! Her love! Her wealth. And yet, after being ushered to his room, his bag having been carried in before him, at once becoming nervous as to the suit. It was damp and wrinkled.

These "althoughs," "ifs," "if onlys," "and yets" are the permanent structure of his doubled world, every world becomes conditional, concessive, possible, yet in becoming possible, impossible. For the very same reason the door is opened, a foot is held against it to open it only a crack.

That Clyde is askew within every world is demonstrated in his helplessness when he tries to connect within a world. He does not know how to find an abortionist because he belongs neither to the middle-class world whose doctors accommodate when a "problem exists" (as we learn from the attorney's story) nor to the working-class world where lore and gossip would supply him with the name of a back-alley abortionist. His life being arranged with mirrors, he has no connections anywhere and ends up in a clothing store desperately trying the clerk's knowledge of "solutions." Later Dreiser carefully shows that were Clyde of the Griffiths world the entire crime would have been hushed up. On the other side, were he an ordinary factory worker no one would have cared. Because the jury can resent him as a well-connected seducer of a poor girl while the Griffiths deny him as "not really one of us," he is important enough to exterminate but not important enough to rescue.

Justice, through the choice of lawyers and legal maneuvers that Samuel Griffiths can buy for Clyde, is a matter of sets and worlds, too.

What is his name? Clyde Griffiths (of the Kansas City Griffiths)? Harry Tenet (his name during his flight after the car accident)? Clyde Griffiths (of the Lycurgus Griffiths)? Clifford Golden or Carl Graham (the names he uses to register at hotels with Roberta)? At his trial the evidence against him consists of matters of identity. How can he explain his two straw hats, the wet suit? His is the first murder in literature in which the weapon is a camera. Dredged up from the lake it contains identifying pictures that along with Roberta's letters that he forgot to burn turn the jury against him decisively.

In *An American Tragedy,* defective membership means not only having no world but also having no self. Deprived of set and setting, having no group which we can say he is "one of," Clyde drifts into the inevitable worldless acts: murder and then execution. Unable to erase the signs of his set through abortion or murder he is caught halfway through the door and imprisoned on the threshold. Literally, death row is such a threshold since the men there are no longer legally alive but not yet dispatched. Like the sidewalk church with which Dreiser began, it is a temporary, self-contained world of fixed roles under emergency conditions. The ever stronger meaning of the adjective "emergency" as we move from the improvised church, to the emergency of abortion, to the flight after murder, to death row suggests the inner nature of what Dreiser means by tragedy. For him tragedy has a circular or spiral quality where each return to what seems to be the same predicament is in fact located farther from the center.

Chronology

1871	Born August 27, in Terre Haute, Indiana.
1879	Family breaks up; Dreiser accompanies his mother to Vincennes, Sullivan, and Evansville, Indiana.
1883	Family briefly reunites in Chicago and then moves to Warsaw, Indiana.
1887	Dreiser goes to Chicago alone; works at several jobs doing menial labor.
1889–90	Dreiser attends Indiana University.
1890	Mother dies.
1892	Dreiser finds a job as a reporter for the Chicago *Globe*. In November he takes a position as a reporter for the *Globe-Democrat* and the *Republic*.
1893	Meets Sara (Sallie) White.
1894	Dreiser works for newspapers in Toledo, Cleveland, and Pittsburgh.
1895	Moves to New York and becomes editor of *Ev'ry Month*.
1898	Marries Sallie White.
1899	Begins writing *Sister Carrie* in Maumee, Ohio, while visiting Arthur Henry.
1900	*Sister Carrie* published by Doubleday, Page and Company, but suppressed.
1901–3	Suffers from depression; separates from Sallie. Dreiser's brother Paul helps him, sending him to Muldoon's health camp in Westchester, New York.
1904–6	Resumes work as fiction editor for Street and Smith Publications, editing dime novels for *Smith's Magazine* and *Broadway Magazine*.
1906	Brother Paul dies.
1907	B. W. Dodge and Company republishes *Sister Carrie*. Dreiser

	becomes editor of *Delineator, New Idea Women's Magazine,* and *Designer.*
1908	Begins friendship with H. L. Mencken.
1909	Dreiser begins *Jennie Gerhardt.*
1910	Fired from Butterick Publications because of involvement with daughter of a woman employee.
1911	Harper and Brothers publishes *Jennie Gerhardt.* Dreiser travels to Europe.
1912	Harper and Brothers reprints *Sister Carrie* and publishes *The Financier,* first volume of Cowperwood trilogy.
1913	*A Traveler at Forty* (autobiography) published.
1914	*The Titan,* second volume of the trilogy, published by John Lane after rejection by Harper's.
1915	Dreiser visits boyhood home. *The "Genius"* published.
1916	*The "Genius"* attacked for obscenity, withdrawn from publication. *A Hoosier Holiday* published (autobiography).
1918	*Free and Other Stories, The Hand of the Potter* (play), *Twelve Men* (sketches).
1919	Affair with Helen Richardson. Begins writing *An American Tragedy.*
1920	*Hey, Rub-A-Dub-Dub* (philosophical essays).
1922	*A Book about Myself* (autobiography).
1923	*The Color of a Great City.*
1925	*An American Tragedy* appears and is a great success.
1927	Dreiser visits the Soviet Union. *Chains* (stories) published.
1928	*Moods, Cadences and Declaimed* (poems) and *Dreiser Looks at Russia.*
1929	*A Gallery of Women* (short stories).
1931	*Dawn, A Book about Myself* which was reprinted with the title *Newspaper Days* (autobiographical work). *Tragic America.*
1932–34	Contributing editor to the *American Spectator.*
1941	*America Is Worth Saving.*
1942	Wife dies.
1944	Award of Merit by American Academy of Arts and Letters. Marries Helen Richardson.
1945	Application for membership in the Communist Party accepted. Dies on December 28, in Hollywood; buried at Forest Lawn.
1946	*The Bulwark.*
1947	*The Stoic,* last volume of the trilogy.

Contributors

HAROLD BLOOM, Sterling Professor of the Humanities at Yale University, is the author of *The Anxiety of Influence, Poetry and Repression,* and many other volumes of literary criticism. His forthcoming study, *Freud: Transference and Authority,* attempts a full-scale reading of all of Freud's major writings. A MacArthur Prize Fellow, he is general editor of five series of literary criticism published by Chelsea House. During 1987–88, he served as the Charles Eliot Norton Professor of Poetry at Harvard.

ELLEN MOERS was Professor of English and Comparative Literature at Columbia University and the University of Connecticut. She is the author of *The Dandy: Brummell to Beerbohm, The Worlds of Victorian Fiction,* and *Literary Women.*

ROBERT PENN WARREN is one of our leading literary critics and the American Poet Laureate. His many volumes of poetry and criticism include *World Enough and Time, Wilderness,* and *Night Rider.*

ROBERT H. ELIAS is Goldwin Smith Professor of English Literature and American Studies and Chairman of American Studies at Cornell University. He is the author of *Theodore Dreiser: Apostle of Nature* and the editor of the three-volume *Letters of Theodore Dreiser.*

DONALD PIZER is Pierce Butler Professor of English at Newcomb College of Tulane University. His critical studies include *Hamlin Garland's Early Work and Career, The Novels of Frank Norris,* and *Twentieth-Century American Literary Naturalism: An Interpretation.*

THOMAS P. RIGGIO is Associate Professor at the University of Connecticut. He has written extensively on Dreiser and has edited *Theodore Dreiser: The American Diaries, 1902–1926.*

PAUL A. ORLOV is Assistant Professor of English at Pennsylvania State

University. He has published numerous articles on Dreiser and *An American Tragedy*.

SHELLEY FISHER FISHKIN has taught at the University of Texas at Austin and is currently Director of the Poynter Fellowship in Journalism at Yale University, where she has also taught American literature. Her recent book is *From Fact to Fiction: Journalism and Imaginative Writing in America*.

PHILIP FISHER, Professor of English at Brandeis University, has written *Making Up Society: The Novels of George Eliot* and *Hard Facts: Setting and Form in the American Novel*.

Bibliography

Benchley, Robert. "Compiling *An American Tragedy*." In *The Early Worm*, 246–50. New York: Holt, 1927.

Bennett, Arnold. *The Journal of Arnold Bennett*, vol. 3, 153–58. New York: Viking, 1932.

Block, Haskell M. "Dreiser's *An American Tragedy*." In *Naturalistic Triptych: The Fictive and the Real in Zola, Mann and Dreiser*. New York: Random House, 1970.

Bucco, Martin. "The East-West Theme in Dreiser's *An American Tragedy*." *Western American Literature* 12 (1977): 177–83.

Campbell, Charles L. "*An American Tragedy;* Or, Death in the Woods." *Modern Fiction Studies* 15 (1969): 251–59.

Conder, John J. *Naturalism in American Fiction: The Classic Phase*. Lexington: The University Press of Kentucky, 1984.

Coursen, Herbert R., Jr. "Clyde Griffiths and the American Dream." *The New Republic* 145 (4 September 1961): 21–22.

The Dreiser Newsletter, 1970–.

Dreiser, Theodore. "Background for *An American Tragedy*." *Esquire* 50 (1958): 155–57.

——. "Dreiser on *An American Tragedy*, in Prague." *The Dreiser Newsletter* 4, no. 1 (1973): 21–22.

Elias, Robert Henry. *Theodore Dreiser: Apostle of Nature*, 218–23. Ithaca: Cornell University Press, 1970.

Farrell, James T. "*An American Tragedy*." *New York Times Book Review,* 6 May 1945, 6.

——. "Dreiser's *Tragedy:* The Distortion of American Values." *Prospects: Annual of American Cultural Studies* 1 (1975): 19–27.

Flanagan, John T. "Dreiser's Style in *An American Tragedy*." *Texas Studies in Literature and Language* 7 (1965): 285–94.

Fleissner, Robert F. "The Griffiths Connections: Dreiser and Maugham." *Notes on Contemporary Literature* 13, no. 1 (1983): 2–5.

French, Warren. *The Social Novel at the End of an Era*, 173–74. Carbondale: Southern Illinois University Press, 1966.

Furst, Lilian R. "Innocent or Guilty? Problems in Filming Dreiser's *An American Tragedy*." *Connecticut Review* 9, no. 2 (1976): 33–40.

Gerber, Philip L. *Plots and Characters in the Fiction of Theodore Dreiser*. Hamden, Conn.: Archon, 1977.

——. *Theodore Dreiser*, 127–53. New York: Twayne, 1964.

Grebstein, Sheldon N. "*An American Tragedy*: Theme and Structure." In *The Twenties:*

Poetry and Prose, edited by Richard Langford and William E. Taylor, 62–66. Deland, Fla.: Everett Edwards, 1966.

Hakutani, Yoshinobu and Lewis Fried, eds. *American Literary Naturalism: A Reassessment.* Heidelberg: Carl Winter, 1975.

Howe, Irving. "Dreiser and the *Tragedy.*" *The New Republic* 151 (22 August 1964): 25–28.

Huddleston, E. L. "Herndon's Lincoln and Theodore Dreiser's *An American Tragedy.*" *Midwest Quarterly* 22 (1981): 242–54.

Hussman, Lawrence E., Jr. *Dreiser and His Fiction: A Twentieth Century Quest.* Philadelphia: University of Pennsylvania Press, 1983.

Kazin, Alfred and Charles Shapiro, eds. *The Stature of Theodore Dreiser: A Critical Survey of the Man and His Work*, 113–26, 204–218. Bloomington: Indiana University Press, 1955.

Lane, Lauriat, Jr. "The Double in *An American Tragedy.*" *Modern Fiction Studies* 12 (1966): 213–20.

Lehan, Richard. "Dreiser's *An American Tragedy*: A Critical Study." *College English* 25 (1963): 187–93.

———. *Theodore Dreiser: His World and His Novels,* 142–69. Carbondale: Southern Illinois University Press, 1969.

Lewis, Sinclair. "The Remarks of Mr. Sinclair Lewis." *Buzz Saw* 19 (1926): 1–4.

Lundquist, James. *Theodore Dreiser,* 85–105. New York: Ungar, 1974.

McAleer, John J. "*An American Tragedy* and *In Cold Blood.*" *Thought* 47 (1972): 569–86.

———. *Theodore Dreiser: An Introduction and Interpretation.* New York: Holt, Rinehart & Winston, 1968.

McDonald, James. "Dreiser's Artistry: Two Letters from *An American Tragedy.*" *The Dreiser Newsletter* 7, no. 2 (1976): 2–6.

Matthiessen, F. O. *Theodore Dreiser,* 187–211. New York: Sloane, 1951.

Michaels, Walter Benn. *The Gold Standard and the Logic of Naturalism: American Literature at the Turn of the Century.* Berkeley: University of California Press, 1987.

Mitchell, L. C. " 'And then rose for the first time': Repetition and Doubling in *An American Tragedy.*" *Novel* 19 (1985): 39–56.

Mookerjee, R. N. " 'Victims of a Degrading Doctrine': Dreiser's *An American Tragedy.*" *Indian Journal of American Studies* 1 (1970): 23–32.

Murayama, Kiyohiko. "The Road to *An American Tragedy.*" *Hitotsubashi Journal of Arts and Sciences* 19 (1978): 40–51.

Orlov, Paul Aurum. "Dreiser's Defense of Self: A Reading of *Sister Carrie* and *An American Tragedy.*" *Dissertation Abstracts International* 40 (1979): 859A.

———. "Plot as Parody: Dreiser's Attack of the Alger Theme in *An American Tragedy.*" *American Literary Realism* 15, no. 2 (1982): 239–43.

———. "The Subversion of the Self: Anti-naturalistic Crux in *An American Tragedy.*" *Modern Fiction Studies* 23 (1977): 457–72.

Phillips, William. "The Imagery of Dreiser's Novels." *PMLA* 78 (1963): 572–85.

Pizer, Donald, comp. *Theodore Dreiser: A Primary and Secondary Bibliography,* 292–399. Boston: G. K. Hall, 1975.

Purdy, Strother B. "*An American Tragedy* and *L'Etranger.*" *Comparative Literature* 19 (1967): 252–68.

Riddell, John. "Blue-prints for Another *American Tragedy.*" In *Meaning No Offense,* 65–72. New York: John Day, 1927.

Riggio, Thomas P. "Dreiser and Mencken: In the Literary Trenches." *American Scholar* 54 (1985): 227–38.

——. "Theodore Dreiser: Hidden Ethnic." *MELUS* 11, no. 1 (1984): 53–63.

Rose, Alan Henry. "Dreiser's Satanic Mills: Religious Imagery in *An American Tragedy*." *Dreiser Newsletter* 7, no. 1 (1976): 5–8.

Salzman, Jack, comp. "Criticism of Theodore Dreiser: A Selected Checklist." *Modern Fiction Studies* 23, no. 3 (1977): 480–82.

——. *Theodore Dreiser: The Critical Reception,* 439–50. New York: David Lewis, 1972.

Samuels, Charles Thomson. "Mr. Trilling, Mr. Warren and *An American Tragedy*." *The Yale Review* 53 (1964): 629–40.

Shafer, Robert. "*An American Tragedy*." In *Humanism and America*, edited by Norman Foerster, 149–69. New York: Farrar, 1930.

Shapiro, Charles. *Theodore Dreiser: Our Bitter Patriot,* 81–114. Carbondale: Southern Illinois University Press, 1962.

Spinder, Michael. "Youth, Class, Consumerism in Dreiser's *An American Tragedy*." *Journal of American Studies* 12 (1978): 63–79.

Stewart, Donald. *American Literature and Christian Doctrine,* 113–20. Baton Rouge: Louisiana State University Press, 1958.

Swinberg, William A. "*An American Tragedy*." In *Dreiser,* 207–362. New York: Scribner's, 1965.

Vivas, Eliseo. "Dreiser, An Inconsistent Mechanist." *Ethic* 48 (1938): 498–508; reprint. in *Creation and Discovery: Essays in Criticism and Aesthetics,* 3–13. New York: Noonday, 1955, and in *The Stature of Theodore Dreiser*, edited by Alfred Kazin and Charles Shapiro, 237–45. Bloomington: Indiana University Press, 1955.

Walcutt, Charles C. *American Literary Naturalism, A Divided Stream.* Minneapolis: University of Minnesota Press, 1956.

Warren, Robert Penn. "*An American Tragedy*." *The Yale Review* 52 (1962): 1–15.

Watson, Charles N., Jr. "The 'Accidental' Drownings in *Daniel Deronda* and *An American Tragedy*." *English Language Notes* 13 (1976): 288–91.

Westlake, Neda M. and Jack Salzman, eds. "An Unpublished Chapter from *An American Tragedy*." *Prospects: Annual of American Cultural Studies* 1 (1975): 1–6.

Zasursky, Y. "Theodore Dreiser's *An American Tragedy*." In *Twentieth-Century American Literature: A Soviet View*, 223–40. Moscow: Progress, 1976.

Acknowledgments

"Pure Religion and Undefiled" by Ellen Moers from *Two Dreisers* by Ellen Moers, © 1969 by Ellen Moers. Reprinted by permission of Viking Penguin, Inc.

"Homage to *An American Tragedy*" by Robert Penn Warren from *Homage to Theodore Dreiser* by Robert Penn Warren, © 1971 by Robert Penn Warren. Reprinted by permission of the author and Random House, Inc.

"Theodore Dreiser and the Tragedy of the Twenties" by Robert H. Elias from *Prospects: Annual Journal of American Cultural Studies* 1 (1975), © 1975 by Burt Franklin & Co., Inc., and Jack Salzman. Reprinted by permission.

"*An American Tragedy*" by Donald Pizer from *The Novels of Theodore Dreiser: A Critical Study* by Donald Pizer, © 1976 by the University of Minnesota. Reprinted by permission of the University of Minnesota Press.

"American Gothic: Poe and *An American Tragedy*" by Thomas P. Riggio from *American Literature* 49, no. 4 (January 1978), © 1978 by Duke University Press. Reprinted by permission of Duke University Press.

"Technique as Theme in *An American Tragedy*" by Paul A. Orlov from *The Journal of Narrative Technique* 14, no. 2 (Spring 1984), © 1984 by *The Journal of Narrative Technique*. Reprinted by permission.

"From Fact to Fiction: *An American Tragedy*" (originally entitled "Theodore Dreiser") by Shelley Fisher Fishkin from *From Fact to Fiction* by Shelley Fisher Fishkin, © 1985 by Shelley Fisher Fishkin. Reprinted by permission of The Johns Hopkins University Press, Baltimore/London.

"The Life History of Objects: The Naturalist Novel and the City" by Philip Fisher from *Hard Facts: Setting and Form in the American Novel* by Philip Fisher, © 1985 by Oxford University Press. Reprinted by permission.

Index